Daniel managed to surprise her

Dear Mrs. Meredith,

I'm sure you agree with me that the time has come for us to make each other's acquaintance properly. Your brother is becoming important in my daughter's life, and although they are both naturally too young for anything serious to come of it, I feel that a meeting between our two families would be beneficial.

I therefore propose that the four of us should attend the dance at Mark's college. I would be grateful for a reply at your earliest convenience.

Yours sincerely,

Daniel F. Raife

Dear Reader,

Another warm welcome to our exciting showcase series for 1997!

Authors you'll treasure, books you'll want to keep!

Harlequin Romance books just keep getting better—and we enjoy bringing you the best choice of wonderful romances each month. For the whole of 1997, we've been highlighting a particular author in our monthly selections—a specially chosen story we know you're going to enjoy, again and again....

This month's recommended reading is Lucy Gordon's *Daniel and Daughter*, an entertaining, heartwarming story about a single mom and a single dad who find that puppy love between their teenage kids brings them a romance, too. Our final **Simply the Best** title in December is a Christmas tale: (#3486) *Her Secret Santa* by Day Leclaire.

Happy Reading!

The Editors

Daniel and Daughter

Lucy Gordon

Harlequin Books

TORONTO • NEW YORK • LONDON
AMSTERDAM • PARIS • SYDNEY • HAMBURG
STOCKHOLM • ATHENS • TOKYO • MILAN
MADRID • WARSAW • BUDAPEST • AUCKLAND

ISBN 0-373-03480-6

DANIEL AND DAUGHTER

First North American Publication 1997.

This edition published by arrangement with Harlequin Books S.A.

Printed in U.S.A.

CHAPTER ONE

'OH, HANG this rain!' Lee Meredith muttered. 'What possessed me to drive in the pitch-dark in the middle of a downpour?'

But she knew she'd had no choice. It had seemed a good idea when the fashion editor of *Modern Lady* had said she wanted the autumn clothes photographed by a waterfall. But the waterfall had been a hundred miles away, and as Lee had clicked the shutter for the last time the heavens had opened. Despite the treacherous conditions she had to get home tonight. She was due at her studio the next morning.

The rhythmic dunk-dunk of the windscreen wipers was hypnotic, and she had to fight to stay alert as she stared into the darkness. At last she stopped at a transport café and had a cup of coffee to keep herself awake. To complete the job she went into the rest room and splashed cold water onto her face. Then she freshened her make-up and drew a comb through her blonde shoulder-length hair, with such vigour that the curls danced. It might seem illogical, since there was no one to see her, but it was a matter of pride.

Lee had found that the company of models could become intimidating, so now she used the tricks she'd learned from the glamorous young women to transform her attractive face into beauty. She was five feet two, built on dainty lines, and presented an appearance of feminine fragility that came from another age.

The inner reality was a shrewd woman who'd learned survival in a hard school.

The cast of her face was naturally youthful, which had once annoyed her. It had been maddening to be taken for fourteen when she'd been a wife of seventeen and the mother of a year-old child. But now, at twenty-nine, there was a certain satisfaction in knowing she looked several years younger. Her petite figure and mass of honey-blonde hair completed the effect. It would be a clever man who could guess Lee Meredith's true age, and he would have to get close enough to look into her dark blue eyes and see the pain and disillusion that she concealed behind laughter.

When she was back on the road she drove slowly and carefully. The conditions were dangerous, and she was too tired to react fast. If only those windscreen wipers weren't so soporific. If only...

She saw a car come out of a side road and swing round to face her. For what seemed like an age she stared at it in bewilderment, trying to work out why something seemed strange. Only after several seconds did her weary brain register the fact that the car was driving straight towards her *on the same side of the road.*

She slammed on her brakes and slowed, but she knew she couldn't stop in time. The other car continued, straight in her path. At the very last second the two vehicles swerved in the same direction, their front wheels connected and they came to a forcible halt.

Lee let out her breath slowly, discovering that she was unhurt. Luckily there was no other traffic on the road. Her temper rising fast, she flung open her door to plunge out into the downpour.

From the other vehicle came a howl of unutterable despair. It might have been an animal keening over its slaughtered young, or it might have been a man bewailing the fate of his brand-new car. The two sounds were indistinguishable.

Through the rain and darkness Lee could just discern that the car was the latest model of an extremely expensive make. It was a beautiful vehicle barring the ugly dent in the front, which exactly mirrored the one in her own.

A man appeared. He was tall and lean, but with his hair plastered to his skull it was hard for her to see more. 'I don't know what country you come from,' she snapped, 'but this happens to be England and we drive on the left.'

'I'm aware of that,' he snapped back. 'I'm English too, and I'm perfectly familiar with the rules of the road.' His voice had a vigour that didn't suggest age.

'No one would guess it who saw you drive,' she said with heavy irony. 'I take it you're not going to deny being entirely responsible for this accident.'

'I most certainly am.'

'What?' Lee shouted above the noise of the rain. 'You were driving on the wrong side of the road.'

'I don't deny that,' he shouted back. 'I merely deny being *entirely* responsible. You had a long stretch of clear road to see me, yet you did nothing until the last minute.'

The sheer effrontery of this took Lee's breath away. While she was struggling for an answer a tall woman in a headscarf emerged from the other car. She ran over to the two combatants and held a large umbrella over them in protective fashion. 'That's better,' she said. 'Now you can fight in comfort.'

They both glared at her. Even in the heat of the moment Lee's professional eye noted that this was one of the most beautiful young women she'd ever seen. But she gave her only a cursory glance before returning to the fray.

'Am I to blame because you don't know your left from your right?' she demanded.

'No, madam, but you are to blame if you weren't paying attention to the road. You could have taken avoiding action before you did—'

'If you'd been driving properly there'd have been nothing to avoid.'

He pulled a handkerchief from his pocket and rubbed his head until he was no more than dampish, enabling Lee to see that he was younger than she'd thought. He could have been in his late thirties, with a lean, strong-featured face that would have been handsome if it hadn't been rigid with outrage.

'May I remind you,' he said, breathing hard, 'that the first rule of the road is to act as if all the other drivers are fools?'

'Well, you said it—'

'And to be ready at all times to take evasive action.'

'You were driving on the wrong side of the road!' she yelled.

'I know that. The point is that I didn't know it at the time. I thought I was on the right side of the road. You, however, knew I was on the wrong side, and should have reacted earlier.'

'You mean I should have done your thinking for

you? Why can't you do your own? Didn't you get beyond the third form, or something?'

The young woman gave a suppressed choke and was silenced by an infuriated glare from the man.

'Why didn't *you* take avoiding action earlier?' Lee demanded.

'Because,' said the man, speaking with difficulty, 'I thought *you* would. I thought you were on the wrong side of the road—'

'Well, I wasn't,' she said, wondering if she was in a madhouse. 'I was on the right side, and you're damned lucky it was me and not a ten-ton truck.'

The beautiful young woman poked the man's arm. 'She's right, you know,' she hissed.

'What?' The man stared as if unable to believe he'd heard properly.

'She's right. You *were* driving on the wrong side of the road.' She turned to Lee. 'I'm sorry. You see, we've just come back from France, where they drive on the other side. We came off the ferry tonight and—'

'Phoebe,' the man growled, 'if you can't be more helpful than that, just get back in the car.'

'Oh, no, please let me stay,' said Phoebe quickly.

'Then keep quiet and behave yourself.'

Lee gaped at this exchange. 'I didn't think men like you existed any more,' she managed to get out at last. 'Why do you let him talk to you like that?' she demanded of Phoebe.

'I can't stop him,' said the young woman sadly.

'Phoebe!'

Phoebe glanced at the man's face and hastily fell silent.

Lee felt she might explode.

He took a deep breath. When he spoke again, he sounded as if he was controlling himself with a mighty effort. 'For your information, madam, this girl—'

'Girl?' Lee interrupted him scathingly. 'You're that kind of man, are you?'

'What kind of man?'

'The kind who calls a woman a girl because it's an easy way of putting her down. It's a pity you didn't let this *woman* drive. We wouldn't be in this mess.'

His eyes glinted. 'Do you really want me to enlarge on the subject of women drivers?'

'No, thank you. You're probably as biased against us on that subject as you are about everything else.'

She had the satisfaction of seeing him bereft of speech. 'Me?' he managed to say at last. 'Me—*biased against women*?'

'Yes, you. Just because you're in the wrong, your reaction is to turn and bully a woman.'

Phoebe's reaction to this was disconcerting. She laughed until Lee thought she would never stop. Her companion appeared to be choking on his own emotions.

'Look,' he managed at last, 'this *young lady*—will you please hush?' This was directed at Phoebe, whose mirth was reducing her to a state of collapse.

'Ignore him,' Lee told Phoebe. 'I'm glad you can find it funny. If I were you I'd run for my life. Someone who looks like you doesn't have to put up with a man whose ideas come out of the ark.' She turned her attention back to her foe. 'This is the twentieth century, in case you hadn't heard.'

'Twentieth century be blowed!' the man exploded. 'Some things never change, and one of them is the way women drive. You were daydreaming back there, that's why you didn't see me earlier. If there's one kind of driver I dread more than any other it's some fluffy-headed little thing who—'

'Fluffy-headed little—?'

'Madam, it isn't me that belongs to an outdated species, but you—the little woman with nothing better to occupy her mind than her clothes and her hair-do. The one thing you've never thought of is what goes on under the bonnet of a car.'

'I think we have said all we have to say,' growled Lee through gritted teeth.

'Certainly. Here's my card, with the name of my insurance firm on the back. Please ask your husband to get in touch with me. Now, perhaps you'll be good enough to supply me with your own details so that we can get back into our respective damaged vehicles and try to give each other a wide berth.'

'Anyone who'd ever seen you drive would give you a wide berth,' she retorted with spirit. 'That's probably why you're such a rotten driver. You're used to the others scuttling for cover at the sight of you.'

Phoebe made choking sounds, but suppressed them under a baleful glare from her escort.

'And here,' said Lee, scribbling on something she'd drawn out of her coat pocket, 'is *my* card, with *my* insurance firm on the back. On the front you'll find both my home and my *business* address.' She had the satisfaction of seeing his eyes widen at this last piece of information. 'And now I'd be obliged if you'd move your car out of my way, because you are still on the wrong side of the road.'

She turned without waiting for a reply and got into her vehicle. She saw Phoebe take her card from the man and study it, then she gave her attention to starting up. To her relief the engine came to life at once. She let it hum for a few moments, and while she waited she examined the card she'd been given. It read, 'Daniel Raife'. After the name was a string of impressive-looking letters.

No wonder he got mad when I asked if he hadn't gotten beyond the third form, mused Lee. The thought cheered her up.

As Daniel Raife's car passed she had a glimpse of him in profile, his hands clenched on the wheel, his face still furious. Beside him sat Phoebe, who turned her head so that she could watch Lee until the last possible moment. To Lee's surprise Phoebe's jaw had dropped and she was staring as if she'd just received the shock of her life.

The next day Lee contacted her insurance firm. Then she sat back and waited for battle. Somewhat to her disappointment she received a speedy reply to say that the firm had already heard from Mr Raife, admitting full liability. By the same post came a letter from his insurance requesting estimates for the cost of repair.

So justice had prevailed when his temper had cooled. Lee put her car in for repair, hired another and tried to feel satisfied. But it was hard when a promising opponent had caved in without a proper fight.

She was also troubled by the feeling that his name

was vaguely familiar, but she couldn't place it and at last she gave up trying. She had a mountain of work to get through and little time to think of anything else. Meredith Studios was a big name in fashion photography but it wasn't yet at the very top, and nothing less than the very top would do.

It wasn't only ambition that hounded her, but also the responsibility of being the breadwinner in her family. It had been that way for eight years now, ever since she'd finally accepted that her husband, Jimmy Meredith, was, to put it mildly, unreliable. From the day she'd earned her first fee as a photographer to the day Jimmy had left her she'd supported him. After their divorce he'd married a woman of independent means, with whom he now lived an apparently contented life.

Lee had been temporarily alone as it was the Easter holiday and her daughter, Sonya, was spending the time with Jimmy. Lee's eighteen-year-old brother, Mark, who'd lived with her since their parents had died two years earlier, was on a hiking holiday. But three days before the start of term they both returned.

Lee and Mark had inherited the same face from their mother, making Mark appear baby-faced and absurdly young. He was a brilliant natural linguist, headed for first-class honours according to his university professors. Lee, who'd left school early, only semi-educated, was full of admiration for her younger brother. But the admiration extended only to his academic talents. Of his common sense—what there was of it—she had the poorest opinion.

Lee and Mark's mother had made herself Mark's slave, and it had been a shock for him to find himself living with a sister who had no time to wait on him and a niece, only five years younger than himself, who had no intention of doing so.

He was warm-hearted, emotional, idealistic and often charming. Lee thought that when she'd managed to undo the results of her mother's over-indulgence he would be delightful. But for the moment he could be exasperating to live with, particularly when he argued with her about money.

Their father had left him a legacy of thirty thousand pounds, which Lee held in trust until he was twenty-one. It was safely invested, and as Mark had grown older she'd begun making him an allowance out of the income, sometimes handing over an extra amount for reasonable expenses. But his idea of 'reasonable' was wildly different from hers, and if she'd yielded to him too often he would have had nothing left by now.

'What's that monstrosity doing out there?' he said when greetings had been exchanged and they were gathered in the kitchen.

'That's the car I've hired while mine's being repaired, following a collision with a lunatic who was driving on the wrong side of the road. He actually dared to blame me.'

'How could he, if he was in the wrong?' demanded Sonya, scandalised.

'No man ever thinks he's in the wrong where his car is concerned,' said Lee. 'He was a first class MCP. I thought they were extinct, but he was an absolute porker.'

'How long before you get your own back?' Mark demanded.

'Two weeks at least. They're waiting for a part. And I'm afraid that one's only insured for my use.'

'Then don't you think,' he said, reverting to a battle that had been running between them for weeks, 'that it's time I had my own car?'

'I do not. You're on a direct bus route to the college.'

'Yes, but the car I've got my eye on—'

'I know the one you've got your eye on and it's far too expensive.'

'It's my money, isn't it?'

'Yes, and I'm going to make sure there's plenty left when you're twenty-one.'

Mark groaned, but dropped the subject and went upstairs to unpack. Sonya was making tea. She was a thin, sharp-faced girl of thirteen, with a candid tongue and a disconcerting ability to make her mother laugh. Despite some routine mother-daughter battles they were good friends.

'The way he goes on about that money,' she said now, 'you'd think he was the cheated heir in some Victorian melodrama. Honestly, he's a pain in the—'

'Sonya!'

'I was going to say in the neck,' Sonya insisted with an air of innocence that didn't fool her mother. 'And he is. It was much nicer when he wasn't here.'

'Darling, what could I do but take him in? He's a babe in arms in the common sense department.'

'Oh, come on, Mum. Mark's got it sussed. That little-boy-lost stuff is supposed to make us all run around after him.'

Lee chuckled. 'Well, he failed with you, didn't he?

He's improved since he's been living here. One day his wife will thank you.'

'I wish he'd get married and move out, like he keeps threatening to.'

'Does he? I hadn't heard.'

'He says if he was a married man you'd have to hand over his money.'

'Oh, I see. Leaving him free to blue the lot on expensive cars.'

'Why don't you let him have a car, Mum? Then he might save us all a lot of trouble by eloping, like you did.'

Lee sipped her tea, glad of an excuse not to respond to this.

She'd been fifteen when she'd become madly infatuated with Jimmy Meredith, and just sixteen when she'd run away with him to Gretna Green. Almost at once she'd discovered her tragic mistake. Jimmy was addicted to the drug of excitement. It had been exciting to court the daughter of a prosperous businessman, thwarting his attempts to break the couple up. It had been even more exciting to plan a runaway match, dodge her frantically pursuing parents, and confront them in the smithy at Gretna Green, defying them to do their worst. But when he found himself married with a child on the way, he grew bored.

He'd discovered a new thrill in gambling. Her father had several times had to hand over money to cover Jimmy's spiralling debts.

The only good thing to have come out of the marriage was Sonya, born while her mother was only sixteen. For her sake Lee had clung to the remnants of her broken-backed marriage, even after Jimmy had moved on to the excitement of other women.

Whatever his faults, he'd been a loving father, and when he'd been fired from his last job he'd spent all his time with his little daughter. Lee had been able to start her own career as a photographer, leaving Sonya with him while she went out to work. She prospered, and by the time her father cut off the money supply, saying, 'That's all my dear. The rest is for Mark,' Lee was able to cope alone.

At last Jimmy had moved out to live a hundred miles away with the woman who became his second wife. Sonya stayed with her mother, but paid her father long visits in the holidays.

Sonya knew nothing of the worst details. She adored Jimmy, so Lee said nothing now, and let her chatter on about eloping as though the subject didn't give her a pang.

'Couldn't we nudge him into eloping?' Sonya was saying wistfully. 'Then we'd get rid of him.'

'Darling, that's very unkind.'

'But it's a fantasy, Mum. It's all right for fantasies to be unkind because they're the safety valve for our aggressive instincts. "It's easier to treat our neighbour with charity in real life when we've just given him a satisfying come-uppance in the privacy of our minds."'

'Who said that?' Lee demanded, for Sonya's theatrical manner made it clear she'd been quoting.

'Daniel Raife, in his newspaper column.'

'Who?' asked Lee sharply.

'Daniel Raife. Mum, whatever's the matter?'

'That was the name of the man I collided with.'

'It must be a coincidence. It couldn't be the same man because you said your Daniel Raife had a real down on women and this one's the opposite. He writes for one of the tabloids and has a page in a woman's magazine, plus a TV chat show, where he gets people talking about controversial things. And he's always arguing in favour of a better deal for women.'

'Of course!' Lee said. 'I knew I'd heard his name before. I don't think I've seen his show, though.'

'It's on during the day, when you're out.'

'So Daniel Raife is on our side, huh?' Lee asked skeptically.

'Honestly. He writes books with titles like *Women Are The Best*, and he talks about how brilliant his daughter is, and how he's looking forward to her being made a judge.'

'Is she anywhere near being a judge?'

Sonya chuckled. 'I shouldn't think so. She's only fifteen. She goes to my school. She's mad about clothes. She thinks it's wonderful that my mother's a fashion photographer.'

Mark had returned to hear the end of the conversation. 'She sounds like a real twit,' he observed.

'Phoebe isn't a twit.'

'What was that name?' asked Lee quickly.

'Phoebe,' said Sonya. 'She's his daughter. Why?'

Lee was staring at her. 'The man I collided with had someone with him called Phoebe. What does she look like?'

'About five foot nine, very beautiful.'

Mark vanished into the next room and emerged a

moment later with a book. He showed Lee the photograph on the back cover. 'Is that who you saw?'

The picture showed a young man with handsome, regular features and dark eyes. Her professional attention was alerted to the tell-tale signs of touching up that made the face bland and uninteresting. Even so, there was no doubt that this was the man she'd crossed swords with.

'That's him,' she groaned. 'And let me tell you, he's a fraud. If you could have heard the way he talked to poor Phoebe—'

'Most people talk to their kids like that,' said Sonya wisely. 'That's not sexism. That's parentism.'

'It still doesn't justify the remarks he made about women drivers,' said Lee firmly.

'But you can't blame a man for what he says when his car's been damaged,' protested Mark. 'That's not sexism either. It's driverism. I don't suppose you were sweetness and light yourself.'

'Well, he had no right to call me a fluffy-headed little thing. I certainly wouldn't have put him down as a man who wanted his daughter to be a judge.'

'He's wasting his time. Women are incapable of being impartial,' Mark declared from the lofty heights of his age. 'They should be kept ignorant—like Sonya.'

'Well, it would be better than knowing eight languages and talking drivel in all of them,' Sonya countered.

He departed without deigning to reply. Sonya murmured wistfully, 'One of these days I'm really going to enjoy kicking his shins.'

'Aren't you supposed to be working that off in your fantasies?' Lee enquired.

'Oh, no, Mum. Kicking his shins is for real life. The fantasy is boiling him in oil.'

Later that evening the phone rang. 'Lee, thank heavens I found you in,' said a relieved voice on the other end.

'Hello, Sal. What's the crisis?' Sally was an old friend who worked for a public relations firm.

'Could you possibly do an extra session tomorrow? Please, Lee. It'll save my life.'

'It's a bit difficult,' Lee said doubtfully. 'I'm fully booked. I could fit someone in at the end, but they'd have to wait a while. Who is it?'

'Daniel Raife. It's for his new book.'

'Sorry, Sal, you're wasting your time. I'm Daniel Raife's most unfavourite person since our cars collided. He'd never let me take his pic.'

'But he asked for you.'

'He *what*?'

'We handle publicity for his publisher. They always put his picture on the back cover. At the very last minute he's decided he wants a new photograph, and he said it has to be done by you.'

'I wish I knew what was going on,' Lee said, feeling frazzled.

'Well, if you take his picture you'll be able to ask him,' Sally said unanswerably.

'All right, but warn him he'll have to hang about. He can try his luck from four o'clock onwards.'

When she'd hung up Lee took out *Who's Who*, not really expecting to find a talk show host there. But

Daniel Raife wasn't just a television celebrity and columnist, it appeared, but a professor of philosophy with a staggering number of degrees. At thirty-seven he'd lived a varied life in which—if his entry could be believed—he'd reluctantly exchanged the life of an academic for the bright lights of the studio.

'Hmm!' Lee murmured cynically. 'Fame, fortune and getting your own way all the time, but secretly you yearn for the life of the mind. Well, it may fool your public, but you're a fraud, my friend.'

She was rather looking forward to tomorrow.

CHAPTER TWO

FROM the moment she started work next morning Lee knew that it was going to be a bad day. One of the models was late, one had a head cold, one garment hadn't arrived when she began shooting, two accessories didn't match and the hairdresser and the make-up artist almost came to blows. By three o'clock, when she should have been near the finishing post, she'd barely started.

'All right everybody,' she called. 'Ten-minute break while tempers cool.'

Gillian, her assistant, started going round with cups of coffee. Lee regarded her own reflection wryly. She wore old jeans and a shirt, her hair was drawn well back and held by a ribbon and there was a smudge on her cheek.

Never mind, she thought. At least she looked what she was: a hard-working woman and not a fluffy-headed little thing. She went on into her office, but in the doorway she stopped, riveted by the sight of the most astoundingly lovely young woman she'd ever seen.

The stranger was tall, with a bean-pole figure and fine features. Her hair was a fiery, natural-looking red and her eyes a deep blue. Lee blinked, wondering why her visitor looked familiar. 'Was I expecting another model?' she asked. 'What agency are you from, Miss—?'

'I'm not a model,' the young woman said, smiling. 'I only wish I were. We've met before.'

'Of course we have. I didn't recognize you at first. It was a dark night, and raining—'

'And you were having a shouting match with Dad,' Phoebe said, chuckling.

'Are you really only fifteen?' Lee asked, astonished. Phoebe was made up subtly, with an expert hand, and could have been twenty.

'I'll be sixteen in a couple of months. Mrs Meredith, I've really looked forward to meeting you properly. I've made Sonya tell me all about you.'

'Yes, she said you were interested in clothes.'

Phoebe Raife had a real sense of style. She wore a loose white jersey dress, and around her neck she'd knotted a silk scarf that exactly matched her eyes.

'I'm afraid I'll be about three hours,' Lee went on. 'You'd be better off going away and coming back.'

'But can't we wait if we keep very quiet and stay out of the way?' Phoebe asked anxiously.

Lee chuckled. 'I can imagine what your father would say to that.'

'No? Can you? What would he say?'

Lee whirled to confront the owner of the amused, masculine voice that had come from behind her. She had to look up to see him, and only just recognized her foe of the other night. He was dramatically altered, not only by the fact that he was dry and well groomed, but because his face now bore a pleasant smile.

It was also the face of the retouched photograph, but, again, it was different. That picture had been of a bland, uninteresting boy. This was a man in his late thirties who looked as if he'd survived a battering by the world and come up still smiling.

The reality had everything the picture lacked—life, strength and character, and above all humour. The features were lean, the mouth was generous and firm, the chin resolute to the point of stubbornness. But it was the eyes that held her. They were like lights on a dark night, and they seemed to draw her towards him as though the two of them were connected by wires.

All this flashed through her mind in a second. Outwardly she retained enough composure to observe coolly, 'I think he'd probably say something about fluffy-headed little things with nothing else to think of but clothes.'

He had the grace to blush, but recovered himself quickly. 'I never said it. You imagined the whole thing, honestly.'

'In my daydreaming, you mean,' she said, through twitching lips.

'Mrs Meredith,' he pleaded, 'I throw myself on your mercy. When my daughter saw your card and realised who I'd offended, she threatened me with dire retribution if I didn't put the matter right. If you don't forgive me, she'll never speak to me again.'

'I set it all up,' Phoebe said in delight. 'I told the PR woman that the photographer had to be you.'

'And then she forced me to come early so that she could watch you work,' Daniel said. 'Naturally I warned her that you'd order us straight out…'

He spread his hands in a helpless gesture, and Lee had to smile. She knew that his apparent diffidence was no more than the easiest way of achieving his object, but his object was his daughter's pleasure, and she liked him for it.

'You don't have to go,' she said. 'But I'll be a long time.'

'You're in luck,' Daniel said to his daughter. Then, to Lee, 'We'll tuck ourselves out of sight and you'll never know we're here.'

Phoebe slipped away. Daniel stayed where he was, regarding Lee. 'I apologise, very sincerely,' he said. 'When I learned who you were I saw how idiotic my remarks had been.'

'I had a similar shock,' she admitted. 'I've discovered that you're famous as a champion of women.'

'You mean you hadn't guessed?' he asked outrageously, and they laughed together.

'Why didn't one of you tell me that Phoebe was your daughter?'

He grinned. 'I tried to, but you shut me up, and Phoebe kept quiet because she was enjoying the joke. I hope the insurers have told you that I'm accepting full liability?'

'Yes. In fact I was going to contact you and say that I can't let you do that. You were quite right. I reacted much too late, so half the blame is mine.'

He didn't answer this directly, but said, 'Had you been on a job?'

'Yes.'

'So you were tired from working. I shouldn't have jumped to conclusions. Am I forgiven?'

'Of course—if I am.'

'There's nothing for me to forgive,' he said simply.

'About the insurance—'

'Why don't we talk about that later? You've still got this session to finish, haven't you?'

'Goodness, yes.' With a start Lee realised that while she'd been talking to this man she'd forgotten everything else in the world.

She showed him a couple of chairs by the wall and went back to work. There were no more hold-ups and she was finished by six o'clock.

'OK, that's it,' she cried at last.

Gillian served more coffee. The chief model, a willowy blonde called Roxanne, began to remove her elegant clothes, assisted by Phoebe who was full of eager questions.

Lee remembered herself at exactly the same age, planning her elopement, never dreaming of the bitterness and disillusion that awaited her. Then she looked up and discovered that while she'd been watching Phoebe Daniel had been watching her, a questioning look in his eyes. His lips curved in a slight smile that was full of warmth, and he looked as if he could see right into Lee's heart and understand everything there. The thought made her uneasy, as though he'd invaded her privacy. She went into her office and began to remove the film from the camera.

After a moment he came in. 'I can't thank you enough for this afternoon,' he said. 'Phoebe's clothes-mad, like all girls of her age, and this has been a great treat for her.'

She smiled and thanked him, but something told her that Daniel had misread his daughter. There was nothing immature in Phoebe's sense of style, and the delicate beauty of her face was given character by a firm chin. Lee wondered if Daniel Raife might yet have a shock waiting for him in the not too distant future.

'You'll have to tell me what kind of portrait you want,' she said.

'Just show me as I really am.'

'But how are you? How do you see yourself? That's what people really mean when they say "as I am". I'll be honest, Mr Raife—'

'Don't you think we've advanced to the first-name stage by now?' he asked. 'After all the other names we've called each other?'

She laughed. 'All right—Daniel. I'm not happy with this assignment. I've seen the current picture on your covers and I couldn't do anything like it.'

'Thank heavens!' he said fervently. 'I loathe that monstrosity. It's touched up till I look like some damned matinee idol. People expect me to look like that and when they see me they say, "My God, hasn't he aged?" I want you to make me look middle-aged, and if possible a little bit raddled. Then, when people see me, they'll say, "By Jove, he's worn well!"'

Lee stood back and regarded this madman who'd erupted into her studio like the breath of life. She took in the lines of his lean, yet muscular frame, the length of his thighs in a pair of well-cut trousers, the breadth of his shoulders. She saw the healthy look of his brown skin, the laughter lines of his face, the gleaming dark eyes with a hint of the devil in their depths, the aura of controlled yet powerful masculinity that made her office seem suddenly more cramped than usual.

'I might,' she said at last, with an air of making concessions, 'manage distinguished—'

He pulled a face.

'But not middle-aged—'

His mouth went down at the corners.

'And definitely not raddled.'

He eyed her as if assessing the strength of the opposition. Then inspiration seized him. He pulled out a pair of glasses with thick black frames and put them on.

'Raddled,' he said firmly.

She shook her head. 'Distinguished. That's my best offer.'

'What kind of a rotten photographer are you?' he demanded, outraged. 'I'm not asking for very much.'

'You're asking for the moon. Michelangelo couldn't make you seem raddled. You don't look middle-aged even with the glasses on. You've got all your hair, and it's kept its colour.'

He ran a hand distractedly through his shiny dark locks. 'You can blame that on Phoebe,' he said. 'I wanted to use a bit of flour at the sides, but she wouldn't let me.'

'Good for her,' Lee said. 'She has, if I may say so, a lot of common sense that she plainly did *not* inherit from her father.'

He grinned. 'She gets her savvy from her mother.'

'Then give my compliments to her mother,' Lee said tartly.

'That lady has been out of my life for years,' Daniel said in a changed voice. 'Something I'm very glad of at the moment.'

Suddenly it wasn't funny any more. His eyes were on her and there was no doubt about his meaning. It was ridiculous. Discounting their first meeting, they'd known each other only a few minutes, and they'd spent those minutes having a laughing, idiotic conversation. But there'd been another conversation going on beneath it, communicating their mutual attraction.

She took a slow breath. She distrusted this man. Not that she knew anything about him, but she distrusted all men, especially those with charm. Jimmy Meredith had been the most charming man in the world—for a time.

'I'll take you in the glasses,' she said.

He didn't seem to hear her. 'Phoebe says you're divorced,' he said quietly. 'Is she right?'

She looked away and began searching a shelf where she kept stacks of film. 'Is that a professional enquiry?' she asked.

'You know quite well what sort of enquiry it is.'

'I'm divorced,' she said shortly.

'For very long?'

'Three years.'

'That's long enough for you to have found someone else. Is there anyone else?'

'No.'

'Will you come out with me?'

'No.'

'Why? Because of the way I behaved when we met?'

'Of course not. It's just that I don't know you.'

'That's no reason. But you're not going to tell me the real reason, are you?'

'No.'

She turned back to him and found him studying his

fingernails. 'All right,' he said. 'I'm ready if you are. Let's get started.'

He left the office and after a moment Lee followed him, slightly startled by his abruptness. The last five minutes might never have been.

They started work. Lee seated him on a high stool and moved round him, this way and that, seeking angles. In the past she'd adjusted the subject's head with her hands, but with Daniel she contented herself with saying, 'Look here—now over there—turn to me—lift your head a little—'

After a while she said, 'How come you let them get away with that awful picture on the cover?'

'I was ignorant about photography, and anyway I was only thirty-three. Why should they want to make me seem younger?'

'Perhaps they thought you looked raddled?' Lee said impishly, and was rewarded with a spontaneous laugh straight into the lens, which she immediately snapped.

'When my agent said the publisher was hassling me to sign the next contract Phoebe suggested a little blackmail,' he went on. 'I told them they'd have to get a new picture for the book they're printing now, or I wouldn't sign again. They tore their hair but I stood firm. Phoebe then said she knew the perfect photographer, and it dawned on me that she'd been pulling my strings like a puppeteer all the time.'

He exchanged an affectionate glance with his daughter. It was the look of comrades who knew themselves to be two against the world. Lee wondered how Daniel and Phoebe came to be alone, and what had happened to the woman who was no longer part of his life. Instinctively she suppressed her curiosity.

She finished the roll of film and said, 'Let's bring Phoebe into some of the pictures, just for fun.' Phoebe bounded eagerly in front of the camera. Lee squinted through the lens at her and drew a deep, disbelieving breath. This girl was a natural.

She took some shots of them together, then said, 'I've a few frames left. Why don't I finish the film on Phoebe alone?'

Lee switched on the cassette player and disco music filled the studio. Phoebe began to sway with instinctive grace. With her colouring and her languorous movements she resembled a tigress, and Lee clicked away ecstatically.

'Fine, that's it!' she called at last.

Mark and Sonya had come into the studio while she was working. Phoebe hurried over, full of excited chatter about her afternoon, and Sonya introduced her to Mark.

Lee turned to Daniel. 'About that insurance...'

'Forget it. The fault was mine in the first place.'

'But—'

'Lee, please don't refuse me this,' he said seriously. 'Call it my thank-you for your kindness to Phoebe. She'll remember today all her life.'

It would have been churlish to refuse when he put it like that. 'All right,' she said. 'Thank you.'

He followed her into her office and shut the door behind them. 'I'll remember today too,' he said, 'as the day we really met. I want very badly to see you again.'

So he hadn't really dropped the subject; he'd only

been biding his time. Lee tried to ignore the treacherous inner voice that said she was glad he hadn't given up so easily.

'Why are you trying to put me off?' he persisted. '*Is* there someone else?'

'No, there's no one in my life at the moment, and I want to keep it that way.'

'For how long? When will you want someone in your life? I'll come back then.'

She was saved from having to answer by the door bursting open and Phoebe erupting into the room. 'Mrs Meredith, when will the pictures be ready?' she asked anxiously.

'The day after tomorrow.'

'You already have my card, haven't you?' Daniel asked with a grin. 'Call me when they're ready and I'll come for them.'

He took her hand and held it for a moment. She found the persistence of that warm clasp unnerving.

Outside the office Mark and Phoebe were deep in conversation. 'Come on, Phoebe, time for home,' Daniel said.

Lee went with them to the front door. She was afraid he'd ask her out again, but Phoebe and Mark were right behind them and in the melee of goodbyes there was no chance for any more to be said. She breathed a sigh of relief as she saw the Raifes depart together, Daniel's arm around his daughter's shoulders. She had no intention of ever seeing him again.

Next day Gillian was lyrical. 'Fancy you actually having a session with Daniel Raife!' she bubbled. 'He's better looking in the flesh than on TV, isn't he?'

'I wouldn't know,' Lee said coolly. 'I seldom watch television. Have you got those pictures of his daughter?'

They studied the pictures together, both startled by Phoebe's impact. 'You must send these to a model agency,' Gillian said.

'I can't do that. Her father would hit the roof.'

'But what does Phoebe want?'

'She talks about being a model, but it might be just a passing phase. He certainly thinks so.'

'Passing phase, nothing! Not with that kind of talent.'

'But she's also overloaded with brains, and his heart is set on her using them.'

'But she doesn't have to do what *he* wants. She's entitled to choose her own career.'

'It's funny,' Lee said, 'but I don't think that's ever occurred to him. Not if it means her choosing something he doesn't like.'

When she was alone Lee studied the photographs of Daniel and knew that her decision to avoid him had been wise. Everything was there: the disturbing mixture of gravity and irony, the suggestion of authority, the hint that behind this lay anarchy. His face was full of fascinating life, endlessly mobile, the dark eyes gleaming, the generous mouth made for laughter, and for something else...

Lee allowed herself to consider that mouth, and how it might have felt to kiss it. She knew that if she'd accepted his invitation they would have ended the evening in each other's arms, and because of that she'd rejected him. The years with Jimmy had taught her to fear her own instincts, and now she was deeply settled in the habit of playing safe. She could fall in love with Daniel, if she was fool enough to let herself. And as soon as Lee Meredith knew that about a man, he'd lost her.

She went to the studio early next morning and packed up Daniel's pictures. She wrote him a brief, formal note, expressing the hope that he would approve of her work, and was just putting the address on the envelope when Mark walked in.

'I just happened to be passing,' he said casually. 'Thought I'd see how you were.'

'That's very kind of you, little brother,' she said, wondering what it was that he really wanted.

'How did the pictures of the great man come out?'

'They're in that envelope.' While Mark studied the shots she telephoned for a messenger to collect them. When she'd finished she found him staring at her in dismay.

'I thought they were coming here to see them?' he said.

The penny dropped. '*They* were never coming here, Mark. Mr Raife said he might come. He didn't mention bringing Phoebe.'

'Yes, but she'd—' He broke off, blushing.

'She'd have insisted on coming too,' Lee supplied. 'Hence your appearance in my studio.'

'Oh, shut up!' he mumbled.

Lee preserved a grave face, but with difficulty. She couldn't blame Mark for being smitten with the ravishing Phoebe. And now that his lordly world-weariness had given way to adolescent confusion, she liked him a great deal more.

At that moment her model arrived and Lee hurried

to get to work. She forgot all about Mark, and when she next looked he was gone.

The house was empty when she got home later that day, and Lee enjoyed a pleasant afternoon, relaxing by herself. At six o'clock, when she was stretched on the sofa with a book, the doorbell rang. On the step she found a special delivery messenger, with a letter for her.

The letter was in a firm, masculine hand.

> It was cunning (but not very brave) of you to send your brother round with the pictures. However, I can take a hint, and will keep my distance. But only for the moment. I haven't given up.
>
> The pictures are excellent. Phoebe is ecstatic about hers. She and Mark are very taken with each other and have gone out this afternoon.
>
> Until we meet again, (as we certainly will). Daniel.

'What's up, Mum?' asked Sonya, who'd just arrived home.

'I think I've seriously underestimated Mark,' Lee said. She described what had happened, giving a carefully edited version of the letter.

'Have you only just found out,' Sonya asked, much entertained. 'What about the messenger you ordered?'

'Mark must have cancelled him when my back was turned. I noticed the envelope gone and assumed the messenger had come and Gillian had given it to him. Fancy Mark thinking up a bit of sharp practice like that.'

'Love makes a man infinitely cunning,' Sonya said, with adolescent wisdom.

'I don't think he's actually in love with her—'

'Oh, come on, Mum! It was written all over him in the car coming home the other day. He was terribly quiet and preoccupied.'

'I didn't notice.'

'Well, you were quiet and preoccupied yourself.'

'I didn't notice that, either,' Lee said, abstractedly, and failed to see the curious look Sonya gave her. She was realising, with dismay, that now it was impossible for her to sever all links with Daniel Raife.

It became clear that Mark's interest in Phoebe wasn't an idle one. He would have seen her several times a week but for her father, who restricted dates to weekends. Lee learned this from Sonya, who received Phoebe's confidences.

'You haven't forgotten that Phoebe won't be sixteen for several weeks,' she said to Mark once.

'Lee, if you're suggesting what I think you are, you can forget it,' Mark said loftily. 'Neither Phoebe or I want to hurry our relationship. Besides,' he added, stepping down from his soap box, 'old man Raife would boil me in oil if he suspected anything like that.'

Lee opened her mouth to protest that Daniel was far from being an old man, thought better of it, and closed her mouth again.

She'd got her car back, but it immediately developed gearbox trouble and was soon out of action again, which made Mark tear his hair.

'You'll have to take the divine Phoebe out in a taxi,' Sonya said callously one evening.

Mark scowled and flung out of the house. Sonya, carefully avoiding her mother's eye, observed, 'In future I think I'd better taste my food very, very carefully.'

'If he doesn't poison you, I shall,' Lee told her, exasperated. 'Now you've let me in for a rerun of the car argument. I suppose I'll have to give in. He's not having seven thousand pounds, but he can have three thousand.'

But when she arrived home the next day Sonya bounded to the door to meet her. 'Look over there,' she cried dramatically.

A car was parked a few yards away. It was solid, ugly, about ten years old, and painted a lurid crimson.

'Who on earth does that hideous thing belong to?' Lee demanded. 'Sonya—no! It isn't—? Mark hasn't—?'

'He has. He arrived with it half an hour ago.'

'But where did he get the money?'

'What money? It can't have cost more than fourpence.'

'It'll get us thrown out of the street,' Lee said faintly.

When Mark appeared she learned that he'd bought the car from the garage that was repairing hers. It had cost him eight hundred pounds, paid for with credit raised against his student grant.

'You'd have done better to wait,' Lee said. 'I was going to let you have three thousand.'

'Lee, you don't understand. I don't want a three-thousand-pound car. I want a seven-thousand-pound car. If I can't have the one I want I prefer that one because I raised the money for it myself.'

Lee understood that Mark's masculine pride had somehow become involved, and whatever she did would be wrong. But next morning she telephoned the garage owner, a man she trusted, and he reassured her that the vehicle was mechanically safe.

As it was a Saturday, Mark used the car to take Phoebe out that night. Late in the evening a bouquet of pink roses was delivered to Lee with a note.

I'd have liked to make these red, but I was afraid you'd send them back. Is that heap of scrap metal safe? When may I come into your life? Daniel.

Lee wrote back.

Thank you for the lovely roses, and thank you even more for not making them red. The mechanic assures me that it is. Never. Lee.

There was no reply to this, and Lee began to relax.

It was exam time. Sonya's temper seemed shorter than usual, and she was unreasonable enough to blame Lee, actually saying, 'Honestly, Mum, you're like a bear with a sore head, these days.' Lee bore this injustice with saintly patience, as befitted a mother at examination time.

'Mind you, it's worse for Phoebe,' Sonya said over breakfast one morning. 'Even though she's so young, she's taking the entrance exam for Oxford, and she's terrified she's going to pass.'

'Terrified she's going to *pass*?' Lee echoed, puzzled.

'Yes. She doesn't want to go to Oxford, but her father's set his heart on it. Oh, look Mum! There he is!'

'Where?' Lee said sharply.

'There's no need to jump like that. He's in the paper.'

Lee studied the newspaper that Sonya pushed across the table, and saw one of her own pictures of Daniel forming part of an advertisement for a book called *Women, Beware Men*, to be published in a week's time. There were the dates of several television interviews.

'We must watch,' Sonya said.

'You can if you like,' Lee said casually. 'I have other things to do.'

In the end she saw him by accident. While channel-hopping she found Daniel's face smiling at her.

'Scientists have known for years that women are really the stronger sex,' he was saying. 'They stand up better than men to extremes of heat, cold and pain. They're tougher too.'

The interviewer, a young woman, pressed him. 'Then how did men gain the upper hand?'

'Because we have the muscular power. You're stronger in the long term, but we're stronger in the short term, which is where most decisions are made.

'I picture a cavewoman hunting for food, millions of years ago. As soon as she'd slain the deer some muscle-bound lout jumped out, bopped her on the head and took the credit for her kill. And we've gone on stealing your credit ever since.'

'But surely that's all over now?'

'Not at all. It's just moved on. Men have used women's new freedoms to make their own lives easier. Always beware the man who seems on your side.'

'But doesn't that include yourself, Mr Raife?'

'Oh, yes, you should beware me more than anyone.'

Daniel gave his attractive laugh, and the interview ended in good humour. Lee switched off, wishing she hadn't seen him. The screen image had reminded her powerfully of the real man, and undone the work of weeks.

It was nearly summer. Mark's college was celebrating the end of term with a dance, to which he was planning to take Phoebe. He returned from a date with her one evening and found Lee about to go to bed. 'I've got a letter for you, from Phoebe's dad,' he said. 'He made me promise to make sure you read it.'

Lee thought she could make a good guess at the letter's contents, but Daniel managed to surprise her. It was an excessively formal document, typewritten on his business stationery.

Dear Mrs Meredith,

I'm sure you agree with me that the time has come for us to make each other's acquaintance properly. Your brother is becoming important in my daughter's life, and, although they are both naturally too young for anything serious to come of it, I feel that a meeting between our two families would be beneficial at this time.

I therefore propose that the four of us should attend the dance at Mark's college. I would be grateful for a reply at your earliest convenience.

Yours sincerely,
Daniel F. Raife.

The name was followed by a string of letters detailing his many degrees. They added the final touch to the letter's suffocating formality.

'He says I can only take Phoebe if you're his guest and we all go together,' Mark said, reading over her shoulder. 'Ye gods! He isn't normally as pompous as that.'

'I know,' Lee said. 'I wonder how many attempts it took him to strike just that note of old fogeyism.'

'Why should he want to sound like an old fogey?'

'To make it impossible for me to refuse, of course.'

'Well, why should you want to refuse? You will go, won't you?'

'Yes, love, I'll go. I've been thoroughly outmanoeuvred and I may as well give in gracefully. And don't ask me what that means because you wouldn't understand the half of it.'

CHAPTER THREE

AS THE dance was a formal occasion everyone assembled in evening dress. Mark's dinner jacket and bow tie set off his baby face, making him look cherubic and innocent. Phoebe, whom Daniel brought to Lee's house to collect the rest of the party, was wearing a long dress of white chiffon.

Lee was in sapphire-blue and knew she looked lovely. There was a glow in her perfect complexion and a sparkle in her eyes that had nothing to do with make-up. It was the prospect of seeing Daniel after the long weeks of self-denial.

As soon as she set eyes on him she knew that every moment of those weeks had been wasted. She'd thought of him so often that he seemed to have been with her all the time. Now she saw him in the flesh, and was struck again by his blazing good looks. Daniel's conventional dinner jacket and bow tie poorly concealed his true self—the primitive male on the prowl, intent on luring the desired female into his lair.

She'd eluded him for weeks, but he'd stalked her with skill and patience, and finally brought her to the mouth of the cave. Now his quiet appearance was telling her that she needn't fear going in; she would be perfectly safe. But she didn't trust Daniel for a moment. He hadn't gone to so much trouble to snare her merely to let her be safe.

The joyful look that passed between Mark and Phoebe gave her a moment's poignant sadness. They were so young and vulnerable in their certainty that their happiness would last.

'Are you ready to go?' came Daniel's voice in her ear. 'I've been trying to attract your attention for the last minute.'

'I was watching them,' she said, indicating the two youngsters, who'd drawn a little apart.

'But you were thinking of something else as well,' he said. 'Something that made you sad.'

'I think it's always a bit sad to see children of that age fancy themselves in love. They're so sure it's going to last for ever, and we know it isn't.'

'I agree. But there was more in your face—a whole history.'

'Shouldn't we be going?' she asked hastily. Daniel was coming too close to secrets she wasn't ready to tell.

The great hall of the college was lit up and lavishly decorated with flowers. The dancing had begun and Phoebe and Mark drifted into each other's arms, oblivious to the rest of the world.

'Why don't we dance, too?' asked Daniel.

'I thought we were going to have a serious talk,' she prevaricated.

'Later. I want to know if having you in my arms feels the way I've been dreaming of it.'

He drew her onto the floor as he spoke, and she went, unresisting. His hand pressed into the small of her back, pulling her close to him, and she drew a sharp breath as she became aware of the warmth of his body against her own. It was the thought of this moment that had made her a coward. Now the moment had come, and it was as sweet-sharp and tantalising as she'd feared. She'd tried to avoid it, but he'd been too clever for her, and her heart rejoiced at her defeat.

Looking up at his face, she knew that it was the same with him. His eyes had a glowing light as they met hers, and she could feel a slight trembling in the hands that held her.

'Let's go to the bar,' he said abruptly. 'I can't hold you without wanting to kiss you.'

She followed him into the bar and they found a small table in the corner. When they were settled with their drinks she said, 'I think you are, without doubt, the most unscrupulous, dishonest—'

'Devious?' he offered with a slight smile.

'Devious, Machiavellian—'

'Desperate?'

'Hmm!'

'I *was* desperate,' he insisted. 'It was clear that you weren't going to give in, although at first I'd been so sure that you would. Call me a conceited oaf if you like, but I didn't think you could have affected me so powerfully if it was all one-way. I still believe that. Am I kidding myself?'

She shook her head. 'No, I can't pretend that,' she said. 'There was something there for me, too, but...' She finished on a sigh. There was so much she couldn't put into words.

'Thank you anyway for not saying I was kidding myself,' he said quietly. 'It was so fast that I tried to tell myself that I'd imagined it. But it was like refusing to believe in lightning. When it strikes, it strikes, and there's no use arguing.'

Lee had a helpless feeling that she was being swept away like a twig in a flood. Daniel was determined to make her acknowledge what had happened to them, and not allow her to draw back into safety. But she made one final attempt.

'We're not children to believe in romantic notions like love at first sight,' she began.

'Mostly, children don't believe in love at first sight,' he said. 'If these youngsters knew I'd fallen in love with you in the first five minutes they'd fall about laughing. Do you know who believes in love at first sight, Lee? Scientists. According to them it's something to do with chemicals.'

'But I don't want to feel as though I'm in a test tube,' she objected.

'Neither do I. I just thought it might make you take me seriously. I prefer to believe that what happened to us in your studio was mysterious and inexplicable—except perhaps as something that was ordained by fate.'

'*You* believe in fate?' she asked, wondering.

'Why not? Sometimes it's the only possible explanation. As soon as I saw you that day in the studio I knew you were going to complete my life. Lee, for God's sake, tell me you felt the same, because I—'

He looked up to find a group of young people edging closer to them, nudging and pointing as they recognised him. One of them shyly asked for his autograph. Daniel gave it and spoke a few words to the others. He was charming, but Lee had to acquit him of basking in their adulation. If anything he seemed embarrassed by it.

'This place is too public,' he said distractedly when he'd managed to get rid of them. 'There's a tiny restaurant, not far from here, where we can talk in peace.'

'But what about the others?'

'I'll tell them where we're going.'

He vanished but returned in five minutes, saying, 'OK. Let's go.'

They slipped out of the back of the building. To get to the restaurant they had to go through a short avenue of trees. Dusk was falling fast and in the shade of the trees it was almost dark. As soon as they were beneath the branches Daniel stopped and pulled her into his arms.

'Someone will see us,' she protested faintly.

'Let them. I've loved you for weeks without kissing you, and it's time that was remedied.'

She too had wanted this kiss. After the first hesitant moment she gave herself up to it and embraced him back. The sensation of his mouth moving slowly against hers was just as she'd dreamed of it, and she wondered how she'd survived the long, empty hours without him. It had been such a waste to keep apart from this man when she might have been in his arms.

When he spoke his voice was unsteady. 'I should have known better than to kiss you in the darkness.' He released her with slow, reluctant hands, and drew her out again to where the light was better.

They walked to the restaurant, two streets away. Lee was glad of the cool evening air on her face, restoring some feeling of normality. Perhaps at any moment she would awaken out of a dream, and her quiet, untroubled life could continue.

But then she looked up at Daniel walking beside her, and knew that nothing would ever be the same again.

The restaurant was almost full when they arrived, but the head waiter found a table for them downstairs, tucked away in a corner. There was almost no light, except for the little flames from the three branched candlesticks on the table.

Lee was entranced. This was the kind of romantic evening out that she'd never had. When she'd first known Jimmy there had been hurried meetings in coffee-bars; that had seemed the height of romance. But at an age when other girls had been enjoying the pleasures of courtship she'd been hanging up nappies in a tiny flat and wondering when her husband would get home from the pub.

Later, when Jimmy had left her, there'd been men who'd wanted to take her out. But Lee had had a daughter to raise and a business to attend to. If she thought hard, there were always good reasons for refusing.

Daniel glanced at her and spoke fondly. 'You look like a little kid let loose in Aladdin's cave,' he said. 'How old are you? Five? Six?'

She laughed at his teasing tone and shook her head, unaware that the dancing movement of her hair about her face was making Daniel's heart thump.

'Tell me,' he insisted. 'I've been trying to work it out. Even in broad daylight you don't look old enough for Sonya to be your daughter. By this light you could be twenty.'

'I'm twenty-nine.'

'But—Sonya—?'

'I was sixteen when she was born,' Lee said. 'I married three weeks after my sixteenth birthday. We eloped to Gretna Green.'

He stared at her. 'And married over the anvil?'

'Yes and no. Anvil marriages are only valid if they're conducted by a minister. Most people do what we did, have a legal ceremony in the register office, then an unofficial smithy wedding.'

'I've never quite understood about Gretna Green,' Daniel said. 'Why there rather than anywhere else?'

'Young couples have always eloped to Scotland because they can marry without their parents' consent earlier than in England. Gretna Green was simply the first place they came to across the border. At one time they didn't even need a minister. They could get married by claiming each other in the presence of witnesses. Any witness would do. So they used to jump down from the carriage and hurry through the first door, which was the smithy.

'Now the old reputation clings. People still think of Gretna Green as a terribly romantic place, where lovers can find refuge from tyrannical parents.'

'I wonder if you know what dreadful, bitter irony there was in your voice just then?' Daniel said.

Lee sighed. 'You can probably guess the rest. My parents weren't tyrannical. They'd seen through Jimmy and warned me against him. I wouldn't listen. I thought I was madly in love. Mum and Dad chased us to Scotland, but they didn't find us until the last minute, when we were in the smithy. We'd already been married in the register office, and Jimmy waved the certificate in their faces. My mother burst into tears, and Jimmy laughed.

'I think I began to understand then what an awful mistake I'd made. But it was too late. So we went through the anvil ceremony "for fun", Jimmy said, although I wasn't feeling much like fun by that time. We clasped hands over the anvil and declared that we were husband and wife. Then the blacksmith banged his hammer on the anvil and cried, "So be it!"

'I tried to believe everything would be all right, but I couldn't shut out the memory of Jimmy laughing while my mother cried.'

She fell silent. She'd already told Daniel more than she'd ever confided in any other human being, but there were things that she couldn't tell, even to him. The accusations of frigidity when Jimmy's clumsy, selfish lovemaking failed to move her, the frightful rows when he discovered that her father wasn't going to support him in the manner to which he wanted to become accustomed, the early realisation that Jimmy had never really loved her, and the infinitely more painful discovery that her love for him was dead—these would remain her secrets until the last moment of her life.

'Now I understand what I saw in your face earlier this evening, when you were looking at Mark and Phoebe,' Daniel said.

'Yes. Phoebe's almost exactly the age I was then, although Mark's a lot younger than Jimmy ever was. And you needn't worry. He'd never do anything to hurt her. I've never seen Mark so slavishly in love.'

'I almost feel sorry for him,' Daniel said with a grin. 'Phoebe's still in the experimental stage. Mark's outstanding chiefly because he's lasted as long as two months. Two weeks is more usual.'

'I envy her,' Lee sighed. 'If I'd been like that at her age I'd have saved myself a lot of heartache.'

'That's what I think. She'll settle down when she's older, but she has so many other things to do first that I prefer her to find safety in numbers.'

Lee chuckled. 'Is she supposed to wait until she's a judge before she gets married?'

'I'm never going to be allowed to forget that remark, am I?' he complained. 'I made it off the top of my head in a television interview and it'll teach me not to speak without thinking. I only meant that I want her to develop her full potential. I don't mind what she becomes—a lawyer, a doctor, an academic, Prime Minister—the sky's the limit.'

'But suppose she doesn't want to do any of those things? She told me she fancied modelling, and she looks like a natural to me.'

'And how many other girls of her age have you heard say they want to be models?'

'Quite a few, but—'

'There you are, then. It's a passing phase. Good grief! When I think how women once had to fight for the chances that my daughter is being handed on a plate! My own sisters had to struggle, while everything was made easy for me.'

'Tell me about that,' Lee said, sensing that here lay the key to a lot about Daniel.

'I had two older sisters and a father with out-dated views. He assumed that his son would need a good education but it never occurred to him that his daughters might want one too. When he died he left what little money there was in trust for me. Jean, my elder sister, got a scholarship to university, and Sarah, the other one, worked as a secretary to help her financially. Later she studied with the Open University and got a good degree. Now she's at Oxford as a mature student, while I support her. I'm helping Jean too, while she takes another degree. Life dealt them bad hands and me a good one, and I think I owe them.'

'So you really mean all those things you...' Lee floundered to a halt, blushingly conscious of what she'd started to say.

Daniel ground his teeth. 'Yes, I really mean them. Although I appreciate that I'm often regarded as a cynical opportunist.'

'Well, that's your own fault,' Lee replied with spirit. 'On television the other night you said women should be wary of you.'

'That was just a neat remark to bring the interview to an end. I mean the things I say and write. I'm not just in it for the money, although I admit the money helps. I have a daughter to provide for, plus an elderly mother and two sisters who are entitled to anything I can do for them.'

'I wish you weren't so brainy,' Lee said with a sigh. 'I read your string of degrees in *Who's Who* and it scared the life out of me. I'll probably bore you to tears. I'm virtually uneducated.'

He pulled a wry face. 'Now you've got me tongue-tied. Because I want to say something that would make you think me an old-fashioned caveman.' He looked at her with mischief in his eyes. 'Should I risk it?'

'Be brave. Give it a try.'

'Very well. I was going to say that when a woman looks as wonderful as you do a man doesn't care how long she was at school.'

'That's a disgraceful thing to say,' she told him solemnly.

'It's shocking, isn't it? I really am very apologetic. Unfortunately, I also mean it.'

'That makes it worse.'

'I appreciate that. You'll have to try to forgive me.'

'If you promise not to offend again.'

'I don't think I should make rash promises. You see, any minute I may be tempted to tell you that you're the loveliest woman I've ever seen, and it would be bad enough for me to insult you in those terms without breaking a promise as well. And if I went on to say that the way the candlelight glows in your eyes is making my head spin, you'd probably be dreadfully offended. So I won't say it.'

She regarded him in silence, her eyes dancing. He smiled back and happiness seemed to stream through her. After a moment he sobered and said quietly, 'I'm not just a brain, Lee.'

She met his eyes and felt a shock go through her as she read their unmistakable message of desire and—what? There was some other feeling and Daniel had called it love. With all her heart she longed to believe him, but her hard-learned caution stood like a barrier between them.

'Was your wife brainy?' she asked, to change the subject.

'I've never been married.'

'What? But Phoebe—'

'Oh, Phoebe's my child all right. But I wasn't married to her mother. I met Caroline at Oxford. I'd just gained my degree, a double first with honours. Immodest as that sounds, I must mention it, because if I'd done less well I probably wouldn't have been an unmarried father at twenty-two.

'Caroline was a scientist, also with a double first. Like me, she stayed at Oxford to do post-graduate work. In between studying we made love. When she told me she was pregnant I just assumed we'd get married. Caroline thought that was hilarious. Marriage had never been on her agenda. I'd been part of an experiment in selective breeding.'

'You mean, because you both had a double first—?' Lee asked, horrified.

'Exactly. The idea was to produce a brilliant child.'

'Ye gods!'

'I expressed it rather more strongly at the time. She was adamant. The child was hers, her own private breeding experiment. But she hadn't taken the paternal instinct into account. I adored that little girl from the moment she was born.

'For the first year things weren't too bad, but then Caroline was offered a job in America, so she gave Phoebe to her sister and her husband, who were childless. They tried to stop me visiting my daughter. They never managed it completely, but there was a time when I was only seeing her once a month.

'When she was four the marriage broke up. Caroline's sister went off with another man and her husband put Phoebe into care. The local authority tried to have her adopted. I had to take them to court to get her back.'

'But what about Caroline? Didn't she take any more interest in her own child?'

'Only at a distance. She sent the local authority a fax supporting me, but she didn't bother to come over. These days I get phone calls demanding to know if I'm educating our daughter properly, and criticising everything I do, but motherly duty stops there. I've taken Phoebe to America a couple of times to meet her, but they didn't get on. Phoebe thinks Caroline's narrow-minded.

'We're happy together: a team. I've tried to make up to her for those first rotten years. I suppose it'll be a while before I know if I've succeeded, but I think she's turning out pretty well.'

In the dim light Lee could see that his face was glowing with fatherly pride, and his voice was vibrant with love for his daughter. She smiled, feeling oddly warmer and closer to him now than she'd done when he was trying to make love to her.

'You don't have to be modest,' she said. 'Any parent would be proud of her.'

'Well, I think so, but then I may be biased.' He grinned. 'I've learned a lot in looking after her. Chiefly I've discovered how fiercely women protect their territory.'

'*We* do?'

'Certainly. You think you're the only ones who know how to be mothers, and if a man dares to open his mouth you drive him off with harassment. When Phoebe was little, I used to take her to the clinic and we'd sit together in the waiting room with all the other mothers and their children. And every woman in the place would scowl at me for daring to think I could do her job.

'Then we'd go in to see the nurse, who'd talk about "this poor little motherless mite". One even had the gall to tell me I should get married "because a child needs a mother". I've been a damned sight better mother to Phoebe than either of the two women who've tried it, I can tell you.'

There was a crash from behind him. Lee, who could see what had happened, rocked with laughter at the sight of two waiters scrabbling on the floor, trying to retrieve the dishes they'd broken between them.

'You should keep your voice down,' she said, wiping her eyes. 'That waiter heard you say you'd been a mother, turned to hear more and went right into another waiter who was doing the same thing.'

She didn't add that it was the contrast between his words and his unmistakable masculinity that had caused the minor sensation. Even she, who knew by now that Daniel was a very unusual man, had a shock when she tried to reconcile the almost womanly tenderness of his love for his daughter with the dangerous virility that radiated from every line of him.

Daniel grinned. 'I'll have to be careful what I say. I've never really talked to anyone about this before. I don't want it getting around.'

'I should think you'd make it the subject of the next book.'

'No,' he said at once. 'I shan't write about this. It's too painful. Besides, Phoebe wouldn't like it. But you see, I've come by my beliefs honestly.'

'Yes. I'm sorry. I must admit, I did wonder—'

'If I was making a very good living out of women

while secretly laughing at them? It's what most people think. I don't mind the others, but I'd like you to believe me.'

'I do,' she said. 'I'm glad you've told me all this.' She smiled. 'Talking to you is like peeling an onion.'

'You mean I make you want to cry?' he asked in alarm.

'No,' she laughed. 'Layer after layer. There's always something unexpected underneath. You don't look like an academic. You look like—well, like a television star. How did a double first student turn into a chat show host?'

'You mean how did I come to sell out?' he asked with a grin.

'No, no,' she disclaimed hastily. 'I didn't mean that.'

'Why not? It's a fair question. It was an accident, really. I was on one of those late-night TV shows that get watched by three people and a cat. I cracked a few jokes and found myself invited onto an early evening programme. I got onto my hobby horse about how schoolgirls are always ahead of schoolboys at the same age. Before I knew where I was I was talking about my own family, cracking more jokes, and it all seemed to go down well. Suddenly the world was full of people who wanted to pay me ridiculous amounts of money to pontificate on subjects I knew nothing about.'

'What do your family think about you "selling out"?'

'My mother loves it. Jean quarrels with everything I say, and Sarah calls me up after each show to complain about my tie.' He made a slightly wry face. 'I enjoy it while it lasts. One day people will get fed up with my face and then I'll return to my roots. And I'll be perfectly happy—if you're there with me,' he added on a suddenly deeper note.

His words, and especially his intense tone, gave her a stab of alarm. 'Don't rush me, Daniel. For me—we've only just met.'

'You're worth waiting for,' he said quietly. 'I think I understand you. You missed out a whole stage, didn't you? You married without playing the field, the way Phoebe's doing, the way a young girl ought to.'

She hesitated. He was right, but she couldn't tell him that there was something else that troubled her. She feared his charm because Jimmy had taught her to distrust charm. It was foolish, Lee told herself. There was no real likeness between this strong, mature man and the feckless, selfish Jimmy. And yet she wasn't ready to place her heart unreservedly in Daniel's hands.

Suddenly he looked at his watch and made an exclamation.

'It's past midnight,' he said. 'The dance ended at twelve.'

He summoned the waiter while Lee stared at her own watch in disbelief. It felt as if it were only a few minutes ago that they'd sat down together but, entranced by his company, she'd failed to notice the minutes pass.

In the street he took her hand and they hurried the short distance. As their destination came into view they could see the car park, almost empty. Daniel's car stood isolated, and beside it were the two young people, talking and laughing together.

In the darkness of the trees Daniel pulled her into his arms. 'No one can see us,' he said, 'and I don't know when I'll be able to kiss you again.'

His kiss was quite different from the earlier one. That had been a little tentative, as though he was introducing himself and wasn't sure of his welcome. This embrace had a triumphant quality, as though he was full of happiness and certain of his ultimate victory. The crushing strength of his arms, the firm pressure of his lips on hers, were a promise for the future.

But her caution cried out a warning. He was taking her along too fast. Instinctively she stiffened, and he released her at once.

'You're right,' he agreed with a sigh. 'Let me straighten my tie, and we'll walk sedately back.'

CHAPTER FOUR

THAT summer was the most perfect Lee had ever known. It was the idyll she'd been denied as a young girl, the blissful enchanted time when love was at its most romantic. There were no problems in those magic days. There was only this summer, this wonderful man, this ideal love.

Daniel's television show was taking its summer break. He'd insisted on a few weeks off each year to allow him time to write, but this year he gave his time to Lee, asking nothing from her but her company.

He squired her about as innocently as a boy with his first love, claiming no more than kisses. She knew he was playing a waiting game, and that later he planned to demand everything from her—passionate love, marriage, children. But for the moment he was courting her gently, giving her space in which her confidence could grow.

Lee refused to look ahead. It was unthinkable to part from Daniel, but equally unthinkable to launch her little boat onto another uncharted sea, however small the waves might seem now.

'I took a terrible battering from Jimmy,' she said once to Daniel. 'I never knew what was going to happen next, discovering that he'd been stealing, finding him drunk, with other women. Since we divorced I've had peace, because I don't have to pay the penalty for anyone else's mistakes and weaknesses. I know I can depend on myself, so I haven't anything to worry about.'

'Haven't you?' he replied, looking at her sadly. 'What about the grey desert of loneliness you're preparing for yourself?'

'But I'm safe,' she said pleadingly.

'And I want you to take risks, because there's no safe place in love, darling.'

Once he grew angry and reminded her that he too had fears that grew out of the past. His were the reverse of hers. He dreaded that she would travel so far with him, then turn aside, leaving him lonely again.

He was still writing his columns, which appeared twice a week in a tabloid newspaper and once a month in a magazine. Lee had started reading them and was delighted with their wit and sympathy. It was like having Daniel there before her, for he wrote as he talked. Even here he was able to surprise her, as she discovered when she found Sonya chortling over the paper one morning. Her eyes were alight with fun as she pushed it over for Lee to read.

Daniel had headed the piece THE WOMAN WHO EXPOSED MY SECRET SELF, and it was a hilarious account of their first meeting in the rain and darkness, subtly angled so that the joke was against himself. He hadn't identified Lee. 'Jane', as he called the anonymous woman, existed only to reveal to him his own hidden side. He concluded cheerfully.

> I've been fooling myself all along. Put me behind the wheel and I'm no different from the rest of my miserable sex: ill-mannered, unreasonable and, as Jane so rightly put it, 'straight out of the ark'.

From here the piece slid into a neat plug for *Women, Beware Men.* Lee read it with admiration. It was funny enough to make her laugh out loud, yet she recognised the serious man who was always there behind the comedy. Daniel was honest enough to accept the worst Lee had said about him, generous enough not to resent her for it and professional enough to transmute it all into good copy for his column. She wondered if she would ever discover all his facets.

At the height of summer they took a cruise down the Thames. On the return journey Lee leaned on the rails, sipping a drink and watching the setting sun turn the water red. It had been a blazing hot day and the air was balmy. A languorous warmth pervaded her limbs, and she had only to turn her head to see Daniel's adoring eyes on her. Cocooned by his love, she felt a blissful happiness that she'd never known before in her life.

Her hand tightened on the rail to control the impulse to touch him. It would have been so easy to reach out and brush her fingers against his neck, and if they'd been alone she would have done so.

It's ridiculous, she thought wryly. You're a woman of twenty-nine. You're falling in love with this man and you're scared. What's the matter with you?

Daniel turned his head suddenly and looked straight into her eyes. At once he drew in his breath with a sharp sound, and she knew he must have read her feelings in her face. Her heart began to thump. She could tell from his expression that he felt the same as she did at this moment.

'Don't move,' he said in a quiet voice. 'Keep absolutely still, darling.'

She obeyed, and he reached out a gentle hand towards her face. She felt the soft brush of his fingers sliding down her neck, then his face tightened suddenly, he gave a sharp exclamation and pulled away from her.

'Got it!' he said triumphantly.

Lee stared at his hand, where a tiny insect was squirming between his fingers. Daniel released it onto the deck.

'It was climbing your collar,' he explained. 'I know how you hate creepy-crawlies so I— Lee, whatever's the matter?'

'Was that why you were staring at me?' she demanded.

'Was I staring? I was trying not to alarm you into moving in case it slid down the inside. Lee, please, don't get hysterical. It's gone now, I promise. Lee—*please*—'

Lee was almost weeping with laughter. She clutched herself and rocked back and forth as the fractured tension released itself in wave after wave of mirth. Daniel scratched his head and regarded her in bafflement.

'Darling,' he said, joining in her laughter without knowing why he did so, 'for heaven's sake, tell me what's so funny.'

'I can't,' she said, wiping her eyes. 'I'm sorry, but I really can't. Not yet. I'll tell you when we're old and grey.'

'Well,' he said ruefully, 'that has a nice, cheerful

sound. It's the first time you've ever mentioned being old and grey with me.'

'It was just a manner of speaking,' she prevaricated.

'Don't be unkind. Leave me my illusions. I didn't know I'd got that far.'

To her relief he didn't mention the subject again. Instead he started to talk about Phoebe's approaching sixteenth birthday party, with which Lee was helping him. They strolled up to some seats in the bow of the boat, and settled themselves.

'There's something I've got to tell you,' she said. 'Phoebe dropped in at the studio yesterday. She wants to hire me to take some photographs of her.'

'What did you say?'

'I told her I'd do it for free, as a birthday present. You know what she wants, don't you?'

'Yes, she wants you to make her look like a model. I'd hoped she was getting over that. Ah, well, maybe when she has the pictures she'll be happy. Thank you, Lee. It was a sweet thing to do.'

'You're not annoyed?'

'Did you think I would be?'

'A bit—yes.'

'But that didn't stop you?'

'Of course not. Why should it? This is between Phoebe and me. It has nothing to do with you.'

He grimaced slightly. 'I suppose I brought that on myself. You don't know how hard it is to exercise a little fatherly authority after all the things I've said and written. The other day I dared to suggest, in the mildest possible terms, that she might keep her stuff in her own room and not drape it all over the house. The little wretch quoted one of my own columns back at me—something about allowing the creative instinct to flower.

'I tried to explain that this didn't translate into the right to break my neck by leaving her heated rollers on the stairs, but I don't think I got through.'

'You probably never said it at all,' Lee mused. 'I expect she made it up and counted on your not remembering.'

'Oh, no. I got the piece out and checked. She'd quoted me word for word. Phoebe's memory is superb.'

'I can see why you're so certain she'll pass all her exams.'

'Exactly. That's why I wish she'd get rid of this bee in her bonnet about modelling. But I'm glad you're taking these pictures for her. I know my daughter's stubbornness. If you'd refused she'd have gone to someone else, and I'm happier if it's you. Don't encourage her, will you, darling?'

'I won't be sending her pictures to any model agencies, if that's what you mean, but if she asks me outright whether she's any good I'll have to give her a truthful answer,' Lee said firmly.

His mouth tightened with a look of displeasure that she hadn't seen before. 'And the truthful answer has to be "yes", does it?' he said.

'Of course it does. She's beautiful, she's fantastically photogenic, she moves well and she's got personality.'

'She also has a brilliant brain that ought to be used in her career.'

'But surely that's up to her?' Suddenly Lee's eyes

gleamed with fun. 'Didn't you once write a piece called BIGGER AND BETTER CHOICES that said—?'

'Never mind that,' he interrupted hastily. 'If you're going to start quoting me as well my life won't be worth living.' He growled at her in mock ferocity. 'Get back in the kitchen and start planning little savoury things for Phoebe's party. That's women's work!'

He jumped as a bony female finger jabbed him in the back. A large, angry-looking woman sitting immediately behind him had heard his last remark.

'Here, you,' she denounced him loudly. 'Haven't you heard it's the twentieth century?' Ignoring Daniel's stunned face, she leaned across to Lee. 'I don't know how you put up with him, dear.'

Carefully avoiding Daniel's eye, Lee assumed a mournful face and nodded to the woman.

'Well, you've got to be reasonable, haven't you?' she said with a sigh. 'He buys me a new apron now and then, and takes me out twice a year. And besides—' her voice dropped conspiratorially '—his old vests do make lovely floorcloths.'

She got no further. Daniel, wild-eyed, was hauling her firmly to her feet. He gave a brief nod to the angry woman.

'Excuse us, madam,' he said tersely. He strode off along the deck with Lee's hand clasped in his, moving so fast that she had to scurry to keep up with him. She found herself taken, perforce, onto the lower deck, which was almost deserted.

'Lee, you *wretch*!' Daniel exploded. 'What are you trying to do to me? If that story ever gets about—' He covered his eyes.

'It won't,' Lee assured him solemnly. 'I won't repeat a word of it, I promise. It'll be more fun to keep quiet and blackmail you with it. Oh, Daniel, I wouldn't have missed the last five minutes for anything you could offer me.'

He started to expostulate but stopped as he looked down at her face, full of mischief. Into his mind came the face of the tense, reserved woman she'd been when they first met. He smiled tenderly.

'Ah, well,' he said, 'if my career crashes in ruins about me, I suppose we can live off your photography. I'm modern enough not to mind letting you support me.'

'You see?' she teased him. 'Being modern has some unexpected benefits.'

Daniel took a quick glance round to make sure there was no one near them before dropping his head to kiss her lightly just below the ear.

'Well, I always warned you, didn't I?' he murmured. 'You can't trust any of us.'

Phoebe's birthday party passed without incident, barring the awkward moment when Mark and Phoebe, seeking to snatch a hurried embrace in the kitchen, disturbed Lee and Daniel similarly occupied. The young lovers saw the humour in the situation; Lee's main worry was Sonya. But when they were getting ready for bed that night her daughter disposed of the problem in brisk fashion.

'Honestly, Mum, I may not be as brilliant as Phoebe, but I'm not dense. I knew all those meetings with Mr Raife weren't just to discuss Romeo and

Juliet.' She added mischievously, 'Not the teenage version, anyway.'

Lee pretended not to hear the last bit. 'You don't mind, do you, darling? I mean—about your father...?'

Sonya considered this for a moment. 'No, honestly I don't. He's a smashing dad, but that's between him and me.' With a gentleness that made her seem much older than her thirteen years, she added, 'He wasn't so smashing to you, was he?'

'We didn't get on too well,' Lee said cautiously. She was almost holding her breath, hardly daring to believe her luck that Sonya was going to understand.

'I've still got Dad. I won't lose him, Mum, just because you marry Mr Raife.'

'I haven't said I'll marry him,' Lee said hastily.

'But you will. Anyone can see you're potty about him. When you started going out with him your temper improved all of a sudden.'

Lee gave her a wry look, then remembered something. 'What did you mean about Romeo and Juliet?' she asked.

'Well, they are. Phoebe's got it badly, too, now. She's due to go to France next week, and she's been trying to get out of it but her father won't let her.'

Lee went to bed thoughtful. Increasingly she had the sensation that a storm was brewing between Daniel and his daughter. She would have preferred to stay on the sidelines, but that was hard because both the Raifes seemed determined to draw her in. Phoebe regarded her as a potential ally because of her job, and Daniel felt entitled to her support because he saw her as Phoebe's future stepmother.

Offering to take the pictures had been an impulsive

gesture that she was half regretting because it was a step towards becoming involved. But she was committed now, and must go through with it.

On the day, Phoebe turned up with a loaded suitcase and Lee went through the contents with her. There were five outfits and the girl had original ideas about make-up for each one. Gillian arranged her hair in several different ways, from demure to flamboyant.

Lee shot roll after roll, carried high by the tide of euphoria at having this marvellous raw material fall into her hands. Phoebe seemed able to change the atmosphere by the turn of her head, the angle of her body or the expression on her face.

When they stopped for coffee she eagerly turned to Lee. 'Is it going well?' she demanded. 'Am I any good?'

Lee drew a cautious breath. 'You move beautifully,' she prevaricated. 'Did you learn that, or is it natural?'

'I took ballet lessons once. I've never wanted to be a swot. I've always done well at school because I can remember things easily, and I like pleasing Dad, but...I don't know...' She trailed off unhappily.

'It's not the same as liking it for its own sake, is it?'

'That's right! I want to be where there are lovely things and nice clothes and lights. I don't want to spend my youth poring over books, even if I *am* good at it.'

Some people might have thought Phoebe's ambitions trivial, but Lee was impressed by the girl's clear-sightedness and her ability to analyse herself. Behind that lovely face was a lot of shrewdness—enough, Lee thought, to give Phoebe the right to decide her own career.

'Couldn't you just fail your exams?' asked Gillian, who'd been listening.

Phoebe shook her head. 'Poor Dad would never be able to hold up his head again. I couldn't do that to him, could I?'

'No,' Lee said firmly. 'You couldn't hurt him like that.'

'For his sake, I've got to show everyone that I *can* get to Oxford, and then get out of going.' She gave a little laugh and scratched her head in a manner that was uncannily reminiscent of her father. 'It's as simple as that,' she said ironically.

While Lee reloaded her camera Phoebe began to study the pictures on the walls. Some of them were Lee's best shots, including some covers for *Harpers*. Others were agency posters. Every model agency distributed large posters covered with tiny pictures of their clients, with details of size and colouring. Like all fashion photographers, Lee hung these up where she could refer to them quickly.

Phoebe stepped in front of a poster from Mulroy & Collitt and peered closely at one of the pictures. The caption underneath read 'Roxanne, 5' 8". Blonde, green eyes'.

'That's the model I talked to the first day, isn't it?' she asked Lee, who'd come up behind her.

'That's right,' Lee said. 'She's one of the best.'

Huge rolls of coloured paper were strung up between posts to provide a variety of backgrounds. Lee pulled the gold paper down until it touched the floor. Phoebe was clad in the white dress she'd worn to the college ball, decorated with gilt jewellery. The belt was a gilt chain, bracelets jangled on her wrists, and her ears sported earrings so long that only someone with Phoebe's swan-like neck would have dared to wear them. Against the gold background, in the white dress, with her pale skin and flaming red hair, she was a gorgeous study in contrasts.

When she'd finished, Lee said, 'Phoebe, I want you to put on the jeans and shirt you were wearing when you came in. Scrub all the make-up off your face and do your hair in bunches.'

'*Bunches?* You mean like a little kid?' Phoebe demanded in horror.

'Trust me. I know what I'm doing.'

When Phoebe had changed, Lee set her against a green background and pointed the camera at her. A cheeky urchin laughed back, so different from the previous shot that it seemed impossible it could be the same person. Lee gave a sigh of pure professional pleasure.

When the session was finished Phoebe changed back into her ordinary clothes and followed Lee into the cubbyhole.

'Do you think they're going to be good, Lee?' she asked eagerly.

'Yes,' Lee said guardedly. 'I think they are.'

'Good enough for me to be a model?'

'That's not a fair question,' she prevaricated.

'Why? Because you've promised my father that you won't encourage me?' Phoebe asked with disconcerting shrewdness.

'Well, you know how he feels.'

'That's Dad's trouble,' Phoebe said severely. 'He

will cloud the issue with personal feelings when I'm talking about facts. Either I'm good enough to be a professional model or I'm not. Feelings don't come into it. If I'm hopelessly bad I wouldn't expect you to keep quiet about that because it might hurt my feelings.'

Lee was privately so much in agreement with this that she was left floundering in silent despair for an answer.

'So please tell me,' Phoebe went on. '*Am* I hopelessly bad?'

'No,' Lee admitted reluctantly. 'You're not.'

Phoebe watched Lee's face for a moment before moving in for the kill. 'Am I good?'

'You know you are.'

'How good?'

'I'll have to see the pictures before I can be sure of that.'

'But you've got a pretty clear idea already, haven't you? If I said I was determined to become a model, would you say I was raving mad?'

Lee ran a hand distractedly through her hair. She'd expected questions, but not this cunningly phrased interrogation. 'No, I wouldn't say that,' she said at last. 'But I would say you ought to listen to your father. He knows the world better than you do.'

'Not the fashion world, he doesn't. You're the expert there. That's why I'm asking you.'

'But he's your father and you're very young.'

'I'm at the age when people normally start thinking about their careers,' Phoebe said reasonably. 'If I said I wanted to go to Oxford I don't suppose either of you would say I was too young to make that decision, would you?'

'I suppose there's something in that,' Lee admitted, frowning. 'I do think you're entitled to rather more say in your own future than he seems to be giving you.'

'Lee, please tell me honestly. Do I have the talent to be a model?'

Lee sighed and gave up. She'd warned Daniel that if this moment came she would have to tell Phoebe the truth.

'Yes, you do,' she said. 'You look fabulous and you're terribly photogenic. But it's an insecure life and a very hard one. You could get ill and your looks could vanish overnight. You could wear yourself out banging on doors trying to get a start.'

'But *you* could employ me—'

'Oh, no, I couldn't,' Lee said hastily, shuddering at the thought of Daniel's reaction to this plan. 'Not while your father's against it.'

'But if it weren't for Dad you'd employ me, wouldn't you?'

'I didn't say that. There could be all sorts of reasons for my not using you. You might not be suitable for any of the things I'm booked to do. You were the one who wanted to keep it impersonal. You're not suggesting that I should show you favouritism, are you?'

'Of course not. But I don't want to be discriminated against either,' Phoebe pleaded. 'If I'm not right for a particular job, fair enough. But you've got me on a blacklist all because of Dad. That's not only unjust, it's restraint of trade.'

'Pardon?' Lee said blankly.

'Restraint of trade. It's a legal concept. It's against the law for anyone to do something that interferes with another person's freedom to earn their living. The fact is, if it weren't for Dad, you'd hire me sometimes, wouldn't you?'

'I think I'd better not answer that,' Lee said, feeling the waters beginning to close over her head.

'That's all right,' Phoebe said wickedly. 'Some people take silence to mean consent.'

'Phoebe, why don't you just become a lawyer?' Lee pleaded. 'I'm beginning to think it's exactly what you're cut out for.'

Phoebe laughed—the young, confident laugh of someone who knew she could make the world dance to her tune.

'That's what Dad says,' she said serenely. 'But I know what's right for me and I'm going to have it, no matter what he thinks. Thanks a million, Lee.'

When she'd gone the studio seemed quiet, as though a whirlwind had hit it and passed on.

'Were you ever that young and that sure?' mused Gillian.

'Yes,' Lee said. 'And it was a disaster. But then, I wasn't a genius.'

CHAPTER FIVE

LEE had no leisure to think of Phoebe for the next few days. Sonya was leaving to spend part of her summer holidays with Jimmy, and Lee's time was taken up with supervising her preparations. Mother and daughter enjoyed a final shopping trip together, during which Lee splashed out on a new dress for herself. When they got home she paraded in it before the mirror. It was blue silk, highlighting her eyes, and cut so that it clung to her dainty figure.

She commended herself for choosing something so classically restrained, until Sonya blew this self-deception apart with the frank comment, 'Jolly good, Mum! It's about time you bought something sexy.'

'Don't be vulgar, darling! It's elegant and simple.'

'Of course it is. Elegant, simple and sexy.'

'Sonya!'

Sonya placed her hands theatrically over her mouth. Lee surveyed the gown in dismay, seeing the truth at last. It *was* sexy. It was the most frankly provocative garment she'd ever worn with Daniel.

Sonya's train left at midday. Lee drove her to the station and they sat over a cup of coffee. As always on these occasions Lee's stomach was churning with conflicting feelings. She was determined never to interfere with Sonya's love for her father, but the sight of her going off to visit Jimmy roused painful sensations. Now she was uncomfortably aware that she was babbling.

'I don't know how you manage to fit in so many activities, darling. After you've seen your father you're going on that school camp—that's the twenty-third, don't forget—and then you'll...'

'Mum...' Sonya briefly laid her hand over Lee's, and her eyes were kind. 'I'm coming back, I promise,' she said gently.

Lee let out her breath, her heart thumping. 'I'm really transparent, aren't I?' she asked shakily.

'Well, whenever I go off to see Daddy you remind me of all the things I'm booked to do when I get back. I'd have to be a lot stupider than I am not to guess why.'

'And you're not stupid,' Lee said with a little smile.

'I wish you'd stop worrying. I love Daddy, but I wouldn't want to live with him. His latest fad is to want me to call him Jimmy,' she added wryly.

'*What?* Why?'

'For the same reason he's started wearing trendy clothes and pulling his stomach in. He's nearly forty and he hates it. It drives Erica mad.' Erica was Jimmy's second wife.

Sonya's wisdom had made her seem mature, but suddenly she changed, becoming again a thirteen-year-old girl, gleefully winding her mother up.

'I tell you what, Mum,' she said with elaborate casualness, 'I won't go after all. I'll stay here and you and I will spend this next week together having a wonderful time—just the two of us.'

Lee gasped with dismay before she could stop herself. Meeting her daughter's eyes, she found them brimming with fun. Of course, Sonya knew Lee was planning to see a lot of Daniel. No one had told her, but she knew.

'I think it's time you got on the train,' she said firmly.

'But shouldn't I stay here and keep you company—?'

'Get on the train, Sonya.'

'I just hate to think of your being all alone—'

'Get on the train before I take you by the scruff of the neck and put you on.' She joined in Sonya's laughter. 'I'm not going to pass up the chance of getting rid of you for a week,' she said. 'It's your father's turn to suffer.'

At the train door they hugged each other vigorously. 'Be good,' Sonya said, and hopped on board before Lee could protest.

Daniel had been out of town for a few days, but they were to see each other that evening. Lee prepared with great care, putting on the beautiful dress, then taking it off, and finally putting it on again. At last she spoke to herself firmly. It was time to stop being nonsensical. She was a grown woman and she'd made up her mind, finally, definitely, once and for all. At least—she thought she had.

Daniel pulled open the door as she ran up the steps of his house, and no sooner had it shut behind her than she was in his arms being hungrily kissed in a way that made her head spin.

'I haven't kissed you for a hundred years,' he murmured when they paused for breath. 'Has it occurred to you that this is the first time we'd ever had total privacy?'

'Not really,' she gasped. 'I've spent evenings here before, when we were quite alone.'

'Yes,' he agreed between kisses, 'but that's not quite the same thing.'

Suddenly there was a violent hissing noise from somewhere in the background. Daniel jerked free with an appalled cry of 'Ye gods!' and vanished into the kitchen. Lee followed just as he opened a window, frantically flapping at the smoke.

'Is the dinner ruined?' she asked cheerfully.

'No, that was an early stage—a minor disaster and easily remedied. Here—' He poured her a glass of red wine and made her stand clear.

'Can't I help?' she protested.

'Menial tasks only. Women shouldn't really be allowed in kitchens. You're all rotten cooks.'

When she saw how at home he was in his gadget-filled kitchen, she had to concede his point.

'You're a fraud,' she laughed as they stood watching bubbling saucepans. 'You told Phoebe she had to go to Paris out of politeness, but you were actually getting rid of the poor girl.'

'She really did have a long-standing engagement with the Bressons,' Daniel protested, 'and it would have been rude to break it. But I must admit I'm glad to have the house to myself for a week.'

'Yes, I know exactly what you mean,' Lee said. 'I felt the same when I was finally alone. Perfect freedom from inquisitive, adolescent eyes.'

'But haven't you still got Mark with you?'

'Not any more. He announced yesterday morning that he felt like taking a driving holiday, and by evening he'd gone.'

'In that thing?' Daniel asked hilariously. 'He's mad. Where does he think it's going to take him?'

'He was very cagey about his destination, but he couldn't meet my eye and his passport's missing.'

'You're trying to tell me that he's gone to Paris, aren't you?'

'I think it's likely.'

Daniel sighed. 'What it is to be young! Only besotted love could explain his taking that contraption on a long journey and actually expecting to get there. Thanks for telling me. I'll phone Madame Bresson and warn her to look out for an English boy with a moonstruck expression.'

While he tended his saucepans Lee left the kitchen, meaning to make herself useful by setting the table. But on the threshold of the dining room she stopped, riveted.

Everything was prepared, including a small round table for two, covered with a cloth that swept the floor all the way around. It was exquisitely laid with silver and crystal. Silver candelabra stood waiting to be lit, and by one of the place-settings was a tiny vase bearing a single flower.

Lee's eyebrows rose a fraction and her mouth moved in a tender smile. Whoever had gone to so much trouble over this room had meant to be taken seriously.

When the meal was ready Daniel loaded it onto a heated trolley and wheeled it in. He made Lee sit while he served her, and smiled as he saw her looking at the rose. When her starter was before her he lit the candles and went to switch off the electric light. The room was immediately thrown into romantic dimness, lit only by the dancing flames.

'You forgot the sweet music,' she murmured.

'No, I didn't.' Daniel made his way to the hi-fi, touched a switch and immediately there was the faint background sound of violins. 'How's that?'

'Perfect,' she said, her lips quivering. 'You haven't missed a trick.'

He'd seated himself opposite her and looked up to find her eyes, full of fun, fixed on him. 'You're very disheartening,' he growled, 'when I'm doing my best.'

'Daniel, I think it's all wonderful, I really do. But I can't see what I'm eating.'

Grumbling, he got up again and put on the light. By the time he'd turned back to her she'd managed to rearrange her face in sober lines.

'What shall we talk about?' he demanded despondently. 'The stock market? The state of the country? You name it.'

'Did Phoebe show you my pictures of her?'

'Yes, I think they're wonderful. And I'm very grateful for whatever it was you said to her.'

Lee stared at him. 'What do you mean? Didn't she tell you what I said?'

'No, and I was tactful enough not to ask. But you must have discouraged her pretty thoroughly because she's been sunk in thought.'

Lee frowned. 'I don't think I could say I discouraged her. I warned you I'd give her the truth if she asked for it, and she did.'

She related as much of the conversation as she could remember. 'I did emphasise what a hard life it is, and how uncertain,' she said at the end. 'But I couldn't compete with her in an argument, especially when she started throwing legal maxims at me.'

'Tied you in knots, did she?' Daniel asked sympathetically. 'She does that with me. Don't worry, darling. She's got it out of her system now.'

They put the dishes in the kitchen and stood with their arms entwined while the coffee perked. Daniel carried the coffee-tray back into the dining room and placed it on a low table by the sofa. Then he pulled Lee down beside him and gave her a swift kiss before pouring her coffee. As he handed it to her he studied the slight frown on her face.

'What is it?' he asked, concerned.

'Nothing. I just think Phoebe's going to give you a surprise. She's as stubborn as you are.'

'Forget it,' he said with a smile. 'I've never had to become the heavy father to win battles with Phoebe. I rely on low cunning. It's far more effective.'

'How?' asked Lee, who'd always found that, however low her own cunning, Sonya's was lower.

'When she was little we had the classic struggle about her going to sleep.'

'And you won it?' Lee asked, wide-eyed.

'It was a push-over,' he declared cheerfully. 'I just used to bet her fifty pence she couldn't stay awake all night. The poor little soul used to lie there fighting to keep her eyes open, and she'd be asleep within ten minutes.'

Lee was awed. 'Now I *know* you're a genius.'

He grinned and poured her a brandy. 'I'm full of dirty tricks like that. I'll teach them to you when we have our children.'

'You're taking a lot for granted,' she said, speaking lightly to disguise the jolt his words gave her.

'Am I? You know I want to marry you, and now I'm in a mood to kidnap you and carry you off to church. I want to see my ring on your finger and my baby in your arms.'

'Don't I get a choice about that?'

He smiled in self-mockery. 'You can choose, darling—as long as you choose me. I've waited, and I'll go on waiting if I have to.' He drew her gently into his arms. 'But, for both our sakes, don't make me wait too long,' he murmured.

She wasn't sure how to answer this, but his kiss made words unnecessary. The pressure of his lips was tender and gentle, coaxing her to relax and welcome him. Yet behind it she could feel the strength of purpose. As soon as she began to kiss him back his arms tightened. His tongue coaxed her lips apart and she let him invade her. Delicious sensations were filling her, making her body come alive with desire. It was something she'd never wanted to feel again, and yet it was so beautiful that she couldn't regret it.

For years she'd lived celibate from choice, trying to believe it was enough. Now she knew that she'd made an old woman of herself too soon, and that it was a crime against her young, ardent flesh. It was a crime also against her heart, which wanted to swell with joy at her lover's embrace, as it did now.

Daniel held her for a long time, kissing and caressing her, gently rousing her desire without rushing her. She had what she needed, which was time to relax, to move at her own speed, while still knowing that he was in control, and she could trust him.

'Lee, my darling...' he murmured at last. 'I want you so much...'

'Yes,' she whispered. 'Yes...'

At once he rose, lifting her off the sofa and cradling her against his chest. Despite her weight he almost ran up the stairs and kicked open the bedroom door.

He undressed her slowly, touching her with reverent hands. In his arms she felt precious, valuable. How different from Jimmy's selfish lust, which had taught her to shrink from sex. But then she banished Jimmy. He had no place in the miracle that was happening now. Daniel's worshipful ardour enclosed her, shutting out all thoughts but him.

When they lay naked together he kissed her body all over. His movements were gentle but his arms about her were strong, as though he wouldn't risk her escaping. Even then she could sense the determined, possessive male behind the smooth exterior. A predator, she thought hazily, but a delightful predator—a tender, loving predator, such as every woman dreamed of but so few were lucky enough to find.

And then the moment came when she was one with him, and everything was perfect. She'd been half afraid that it would feel strange and unwelcome, that her own fear might cause the ultimate union to destroy the love that had been quietly growing between them. But now all fear fled away. How could it feel strange to love Daniel when he understood her so well and cared for her with such sensitivity? His concern was all for her.

She could feel the effort it cost him to leash back his own passion until she was ready, but he didn't fail her. She had a glorious sense of ease, of relaxing even in the midst of mounting excitement, and when the final moment came she yielded to it readily, knowing that this was right as nothing in her life had been right before. The cry she gave was not only of passion, but also of wonder and gratitude.

He held her for a long time, kissing her tenderly until her flesh had stopped quivering and some of her shattered sensations were restored to normal.

'Are you all right, darling?' he whispered.

'Perfectly all right—and so happy,' she said in a choking voice.

'I warned you, didn't I?' he said with his gentle, heart-stopping smile. 'I'm ruthless when it comes to getting what I want.' He ran his hand down until his fingers were caressing the satin skin of her flat stomach. 'Who knows?' he mused wistfully. 'I might already have you in my net?'

'No,' she said gently. 'Don't build up your hopes, Daniel. I'm not pregnant.'

'You can't really be sure of that.'

'Yes, I can. Completely sure.'

He pulled back a little and looked down at her appraisingly. 'I didn't really take you by surprise at all, did I?' he asked at last.

'Not a bit.'

'You came prepared?'

'That's right. I had a few last-minute qualms tonight, but I made my decision days ago.'

'Which means I'm not the wily seducer I was priding myself on being?'

''Fraid not!'

His fingers were still tracing a gentle path in circles

that narrowed down as they neared the tops of her legs. His eyes were alight with self-mocking humour.

'To think of all the trouble I went to tonight—soft lights, sweet music. And all the time I was trying to lure you into my trap you were actually two steps ahead of me, wondering why I was taking so long.'

Lee joined in his laughter and shifted her position slightly so that his fingers naturally found their way home. She stretched luxuriously and slipped her arms round his neck before saying, 'Let's say I made my own choice. I'm here because it's where I want to be.'

'Ah...' His murmur was so soft that she had to strain to hear it. 'Your own choice—I'm so glad. Lee, my darling, I'm so very, very glad.'

CHAPTER SIX

THE week that followed passed far too quickly for Lee. She moved in to Daniel's home and began to learn the kind of person he was. The years with Jimmy hadn't taught her that a man could be passionate and funny, fierce and tender, authoritative and humble. It was like being a girl again, in love for the first time, knowing that life would never be the same now this one man had drawn back the curtain on a new world.

They slept wrapped in each other's arms and Lee would awake with her head resting on his smooth brown chest. It was the sensation of warmth and safety that struck her first. Daniel's arms tight about her always made her feel as though nothing could go wrong with her world.

He delighted in getting up first and bringing her a cup of tea. He would hover while she sipped it, enquire, 'Is madam satisfied?' then hurry away to start the breakfast. Being waited on made her feel like a queen. Sonya had sometimes done so, on birthdays and Mother's Day, but as Sonya cooked with one eye on the stove and the other in a book the results weren't encouraging. Daniel gave all his loving attention to creating tempting dishes for his lady.

Although she had the week off, Lee kept in touch with Gillian, checking on the bookings that were coming in.

'Can't you forget work for five minutes?' Daniel complained. 'Relax.'

'I'll never relax until I get where I want to be,' Lee insisted.

'And where's that?'

'At the top. The very top. I get a lot of big commissions but I don't get the top rates, and I'm not first in the queue.' She sighed. 'I guess I'll just have to keep plugging away.'

'Plugging away isn't always the answer,' Daniel said thoughtfully.

'Then what is?'

'You need something extra to get your name known outside the circle of commissioning editors. If you were to win fifty million on the lottery everyone would queue up to have you take their pictures, just to say they'd met you.'

Lee chuckled. 'And why would I be taking pictures if I'd won fifty million?'

'Well, that's the flaw in the argument, of course, but you get the idea. You've got to make people want to say they've met you.'

'Fine. Any suggestions?'

'I'll work on it. But later.' He took her in his arms. 'Just now I have other ideas.'

She discovered that Daniel was a demon cook, with a well-stocked freezer and a library of recipes.

'Cooking for a growing child taught me some self-defence techniques,' he confessed. The trouble is, I became *too* good. Phoebe never bothered to learn. Why should she when her old man can do it for her?'

'Why should she *anyway*?' Lee asked impishly. 'Just because she's a girl?'

'Nonsense! If I can do it, she can do it. That's equality.' He struck an attitude. 'It's time men were liberated from the kitchen sink. Give us freedom! Value us for our brains.'

'Hang your brains! Give me your body,' Lee said, kissing him ruthlessly.

He put up a half-hearted struggle, protesting, 'That's all very well, but what happens when my hair falls out and my waistline expands?'

'Then I shall get me a toy-boy,' she said, silencing further argument.

Afterwards she was never able to remember details of that glorious time. They became a blur of days spent getting up late, picnicking at midnight, and discovering each other in endless passionate hours.

Some of Daniel's shows were being re-run on afternoon television. Lee watched them eagerly. She'd seen one or two before but not as many as she would have liked. As the programme went out during the day she had to tape it, and in the evening she was usually too occupied with the man himself to have time for his screen image.

Now she could study him, and realise what a consummate professional he was. He could work a crowd as skilfully as any showman, making it look easy.

'With so much happening, don't you ever lose track?' she asked one day. 'Or get nervous?'

'I used to. Then I discovered the secret was to have everything at my fingertips and always be in control.'

He was the reverse of conceited, judging his screen self ruthlessly. 'I lost it there,' he admitted. 'I shouldn't have let that woman go on so long—and here the argument got derailed and I didn't pull it back fast enough.'

'You looked fine to me.'

'That's sweet of you, darling, but you don't know anything about it.' He wasn't being deliberately rude. He was just a professional fixing a laser gaze on his own work and refusing to be distracted. *'Fool!'* he suddenly yelled at his screen self. 'I don't know why anyone employs you.'

'Do you normally shout abuse at yourself?' she asked, laughing.

'Always.' He grinned self-consciously. 'I see so many things that could be improved.'

'But you can't be in control of every little detail.'

'You can try. There, thank heavens, it's over! We won't have to watch that idiot any more. Come on, woman. Baked beans on toast.'

There were moments of comedy too. Through telephone calls they were able to follow the progress of Mark's disastrous journey to Paris. He managed to get as far as the Dover ferry, but when the boat had crossed the water and docked at Calais the car refused to start. In the end it was ferried back and forth three times, with the shipping company growing increasingly irate.

Finally a tow was arranged on the French side of the water and the car was deposited in a Calais garage. There followed four days of mounting frustration and lively discussions with the mechanic, in the course of which Mark enriched his French vocabulary with a number of pungent phrases that were unlikely to be of use in academic circles.

He finally reached Paris the day before Phoebe was

due to leave. Sensing what was coming, Daniel made a frantic call to Madame Bresson, begging her to ensure that Phoebe returned by air and not 'with that young maniac and his collection of welded safety pins'. After that the telephone lines hummed. Phoebe called her father to protest at his high-handedness. Daniel, who was terrified for his daughter's safety, responded by laying down the law in a manner that would have amazed his public.

The next day Phoebe flew home. In a terse scene Daniel further demolished his reputation in his daughter's eyes by flatly forbidding her to set foot in Mark's old car ever again. Phoebe set her chin stubbornly at this edict, but was deprived of the chance to defy it by the fact that Mark didn't get home for another three days, having broken down again at Dover.

Phoebe's return was the signal for Lee to depart. Daniel set out for the airport to meet his daughter while Lee drove home, a heavy ache in her heart. Daniel and Phoebe were going to spend a week with his family in the Midlands. Their parting had been a painful wrench that left her fighting back tears. She tried to tell herself that she was being absurd. She would see him again soon. But it wouldn't be the same as the blissful world where there had been only each other.

He called her that night and they had a long, loving talk. But when the call was over the house was very quiet and the sadness lay on her heart like a weight. The golden, enchanted time was over, and who could tell if she would ever know such happiness again?

It was a relief when the young people returned.

Mark could talk of nothing but his misfortunes, and Lee and Sonya had to hear the story several times.

'So you'll just have to get a decent car,' Lee said sympathetically at last. 'That offer of three thousand pounds is still open.'

'Oh, hell, Lee! Why can't you be reasonable now and let me have the seven thousand?' he snapped. 'If I had a really good car it would impress Mr Raife no end.'

'Only if it was safe. And you can be just as safe on three thousand as you can on seven.'

'If it comes to that, you can be perfectly safe in a one-thousand-pound car if you choose it properly,' Sonya remarked, stirring the embers of discontent with an enthusiastic hand. 'Honestly, Mark, how could you be such a dozy prawn as to buy that thing just because it was the first one you saw?'

'That's enough!' said Lee, quelling the incipient riot. 'Sonya, if you can't be any more helpful than that, try keeping quiet.'

'Sorry, Mum.' Sonya subsided, cheerful at having added her mite to the proceedings.

'That car *is* safe,' Mark said furiously. 'The gearbox is almost new, and the brakes never fail—'

'I shouldn't think they get the chance if you can't start it,' Sonya observed cheekily.

'I'm just saying those brakes never let me down. One touch and they're solid.'

'That's probably why you can't start it. The brakes are still on—'

'Now look, you little brat—'

'Shut up, the pair of you!' Lee said in exasperation. 'There's no point in going on about this now. Mark,

think about that offer. Three thousand pounds is all you need. In the meantime, when Phoebe comes back, if you want to take her out, you can borrow my car.'

She was guiltily aware that her fuse had shortened abruptly because she was miserable. She missed Daniel desperately. Offering her car to Mark had been an act of pure self-interest. The thought of Phoebe remaining home every evening, never allowing her a moment alone with Daniel, was unendurable.

I wonder if it'll be like this until she goes to university? she thought. And even then, now Sonya's home, it's going to be a terrible problem getting some time alone together. Unless...

Unless she married Daniel. Then everything would become simple. She managed to push the decision aside for the moment. She wasn't yet ready to take that final step. But she knew she'd moved one important stage nearer.

If she'd had to define what was holding her back Lee would have said that Daniel was too perfect. His charm never failed him, his good humour was never seriously disturbed, his manners were delightful.

She knew she was being illogical, since the first time she'd met him he'd been in a raging temper, but, as Mark had said, that was 'driverism' and in a special category. It didn't tell her what she wanted to know.

All his life Daniel had been favoured by the gods. His brains, his looks, his personal magnetism had combined to create for him a climate in which he generally got what he wanted—often because people were falling over themselves to give it to him. Even the battle for Phoebe, painful though it had been at the time, had finally gone his way. Phoebe herself was a daughter any man might be proud of. Why shouldn't Daniel Raife be charming?

Only when his delightful surface had been shattered by something more serious than a dented car would she know if she could live with him.

She longed for the courage to match Daniel's whole-hearted willingness to commit himself to her. But she'd learned caution in a hard and bitter school, and it was too late to free herself of it now.

One afternoon, when Phoebe and Daniel had been home a week, Lee was getting through her work as briskly as possible. She and Daniel were going out, and she wanted to leave the studio promptly. But at the last minute the phone rang. The caller turned out to be Brenda Mulroy, the senior partner in the model agency Mulroy & Collitt.

'Hello, Brenda. What can I do for you?'

'You've already done it,' boomed the other woman's deep, cheerful voice. 'You really do have a genius as a talent-spotter, Lee. Bless you for sending her to us.'

'Sending who?' asked Lee, bewildered.

'Phoebe Raife, of course. Those pictures are fantastic.'

'What?'

'Don't tell me you've already forgotten giving her our address?'

'Brenda, please—I don't know what you're talking about.'

'Didn't you take those pictures of Phoebe Raife?'

Lee sat down abruptly. Some glimmering of the awful truth was getting through to her, but her mind refused to accept it. 'Yes, I took the pictures,' she said. 'Tell me what's happened. How did you get them?'

'They arrived in the post. When we saw them we couldn't believe our eyes. I phoned her and she came in this morning. Phoebe Raife is now represented by Mulroy & Collitt.'

'Do you mean she's actually signed something?' Lee asked, feeling her mouth go dry.

'No point, my dear. She's a minor. Besides, I don't like to feel our models only stay with us because they're tied up with legal strings. Trust is nicer.'

That was true, Lee thought, frantically clutching at straws. If there was one crumb of comfort in this business it was that Phoebe could hardly have gone to a better agency.

'Anyway,' Brenda boomed on, 'I thought you'd be pleased, seeing as you brought it all about. A little bird tells me you're practically part of the family.'

'I'll be the skeleton in the cupboard after this,' Lee said frantically. 'Brenda, this is awful. Phoebe's going to Oxford.'

'Not according to her.'

'But you can't do this. I took those pictures as a birthday present for her. It was entirely private. They weren't meant to be used professionally.'

'You mean you didn't send her to us?'

'Of course I didn't. I don't even know how she knew that you— Oh, ye gods! Yes, I do!' Lee covered her eyes as the memory of Phoebe studying Roxanne's picture came back to her. 'Brenda, *please*, it was an accident. You mustn't take her on.'

'Lee, dear, I don't want to be obnoxious, but that's

really between Phoebe and me. Whatever you meant her to do, she was free to come to us if she wanted. And modelling is obviously what she does want.'

Lee tore her hair. Brenda was right. She had no jurisdiction over Phoebe. And in different circumstances she would have congratulated the girl on her marvellous luck in being taken on by one of the best agencies in the business.

But none of this counted with Lee beside the inner conviction that Daniel was going to blame her.

She pulled herself together long enough to bid Brenda goodbye. As she replaced the receiver her eyes fell on a scrap of paper on the desk. It was a message in Gillian's writing.

> 4.40 p.m. Daniel Raife phoned. Change of plan for tonight. Go straight to his house. Urgent. He said you'd understand. G.

Gillian returned at that moment. 'Oh good, you got it. I asked him if he wanted to talk to you, and he said. ''No, just tell her!'''

'How did he sound?'

'Not friendly, to be honest. You two haven't had a row, have you?'

'Not yet, but it's coming.'

Daniel's front door opened as soon as Lee arrived, showing that he'd been waiting for her. He was scowling. 'Now see what your interference has led to,' he snapped.

'*My—?* Now wait a minute, Daniel. I knew nothing

about this until half an hour ago. Phoebe sent the agency those pictures herself.'

'And how did she know where to send them?'

'She saw one of their posters on my studio wall.'

'I seem to remember your promising me that this wouldn't happen,' Daniel said, tight-lipped.

'I promised that *I* wouldn't send the pictures out, but I had no power to stop Phoebe doing anything she wanted.'

'You could have taken the poster down. Then she wouldn't have known how to go about this mad caper.'

Lee groaned. 'Honestly, Daniel, I don't understand how you can know so little about Phoebe. Or rather, you do know her but you don't use what you know.'

They'd gone into the front room. Despite his temper Daniel poured Lee a glass of her favourite dry sherry. As she began to sip it he said, 'Are you going to explain that cryptic remark?'

'You told me yourself how determined Phoebe is. She's just like you as you must have been when you were fighting to get custody of her. Any other man would have given up, but not you. Not with that chin. Well, have a look at Phoebe's chin some time. You'll find it's like looking in the mirror.'

Daniel gave a faint grunt of laughter. He suppressed it at once and the scowl returned to his face, but Lee knew the comparison hadn't displeased him.

'What Phoebe wants, she *wants*,' Lee resumed. 'And what she wants is to be a model. You'd have to lock her up to stop her.'

Daniel didn't answer this directly. He left the room and went into his study. When he returned he was holding a paper which he held out to Lee. Her eyes widened as she read the contents.

'A scholarship to Oxford. Phoebe's a young genius,' she breathed. 'When did this arrive?'

'This morning, while Phoebe was out. When she came back she told me she'd spent the morning with Mulroy & Collitt, that they'd taken her on and that she was starting work as soon as possible.'

'Didn't this make any difference?'

'She said she wouldn't be seen dead at Oxford,' Daniel said bitterly.

Lee felt a pang of pity for him. His face was haggard at the memory of Phoebe's dismissive words. Daniel had dreamed of this moment for years, and now the daughter he adored had hurled it back in his face.

'Darling, I'm sorry,' Lee said helplessly. 'I think Phoebe's quite mad, but—'

'Well, I'm very interested to hear that,' he said with a return of anger, 'considering that you, more than anyone, have helped to bring about this disaster. Phoebe asked your advice. You could have put a stop to it, there and then—'

'By lying to her? By telling her she had no talent when she's actually one of the most dazzling girls I've seen in years? Oh, no, Daniel. Not even for you.'

'*Thank you!* That tells me where I stand, I suppose.'

'I warned you that I'd tell her the truth if she asked for it.'

'Lee, let me tell you something. When someone you love stabs you in the back, it is *not* made more acceptable by the fact that she warned you in advance.'

White-faced, Lee stared at him, wondering if this was the same gentle, endearing man she'd thought she knew. Daniel's face was hard and set with fury, and he'd quickly reached a stage where he no longer cared—or even knew—what he was saying.

'I'm not taking that from you,' she said at last. 'I've never stabbed you in the back and I'm damned if I'm going to stay here and be abused.' She slammed her glass down and turned to the door. 'You can call me when you feel able to talk in a civilised fashion.'

She'd got only two steps before Daniel's arm came out and stopped her. 'All right,' he said in a curt voice. 'I shouldn't have said that. I apologise.'

Lee turned back into the room. There was nothing else to do since Daniel was between her and the door. His apology hadn't improved the atmosphere since plainly it had only been a formality to prevent her leaving.

'You must see that I couldn't have lied to her about how good she is,' she said in a placating voice.

'It's a matter of opinion, isn't it?' Daniel said, tight-lipped. '*You* think she's talented—'

'So do Mulroy & Collitt, who've seen models come and go. And my opinion is a professional one. I have my ethics too, you know. Phoebe knew you were peering over my shoulder. If I'd given her the thumbs-down she'd simply have gone elsewhere for an unbiased opinion.'

He made a sound that was perilously near a snort.

'Be reasonable, Daniel,' Lee pleaded. 'You're so proud of her intelligence, you shouldn't be surprised if she uses it to get her own way—just as you do. You couldn't have stopped her discovering her own talents and nor should you try. You once talked about her fulfilling her potential, but she has more than one potential and you have no right to dictate to her which one she fulfils.'

'I'm acting for her own good—'

'That's a hoary old excuse. You should be ashamed to use it.' Lee stood back and regarded him wryly. 'The "women's champion" is a bit of a fraud really, isn't he?'

'For the love of heaven, will you forget all that stuff?' Daniel roared. 'This is reality. I'm not just talking about Phoebe's talents as a clothes-horse. Before she stormed out of here today we had the grandfather of all rows, in the course of which she let slip that you'd told her she was entitled to decide her future for herself.'

'Well, she is! She has plenty of common sense—a lot more than her father, if you ask me.'

'I did *not* ask you, however, and I want you to stop undermining my authority with my daughter.'

'You mean, don't encourage her to differ from you,' Lee said indignantly. 'No one's allowed to express an opinion that contradicts yours in case your daughter starts to suspect that you could be wrong. But she already knows that. She's only gone through this academic charade to please you. And that's as traditional as anything I ever heard.'

'That is utter nonsense!'

'For heaven's sake!' she cried. 'Let the girl do what she likes with her life. That's what freedom means.'

'My daughter has total freedom, but she's not old enough to make the best use of it and so—'

'In other words, she has freedom to do what *you*

want her to. Real freedom means making her own decisions. It's not wanting to become a judge; it's being able to become a judge *if she wants to.* It must be *her* choice.'

'So it will be, when she's old enough to make one.'

'If modelling's the right career for her, she'll do as well starting at sixteen as any other age.'

'You made your decision at sixteen, didn't you?' he snapped. 'Was that the right one?'

She drew a long, painful breath. 'That's unforgivable, Daniel. To drag up private matters that I told you about because I trusted you—'

'I trusted you as well, Lee, and I think you've betrayed that trust. Because of your interference Phoebe can defy me. At sixteen she's legally entitled to leave home as long as she can show that she can support herself. She won't have any trouble proving that now she's on this agency's books, will she? Plus all the work she'll be getting from you.'

'She won't necessarily get any work from me—'

'Oh, come on,' he cried derisively. 'You're not going to let the others use your discovery while you—'

Daniel's voice trailed into silence as he found himself confronting empty air. Lee had walked out.

CHAPTER SEVEN

So now she knew what she'd wanted to know about Daniel Raife, Lee thought sadly as she lay awake that night. And the answer was at least as unpleasant as she'd feared.

Daniel was used to having his own way in all things, and subconsciously he'd come to expect it as a right. Now Phoebe, with Lee's unwitting help, had stood up to him and said no. The façade of sweet reason had cracked with a swiftness that would have been comic in any other circumstances. Behind it stood revealed an old-fashioned bull male, bellowing with rage at being defied.

Lee sighed and told herself that she ought to be reasonable. She herself was far from perfect, and it wasn't fair of her to demand perfection from Daniel. But she found that reason was useless to ease an aching heart. She wondered if Daniel was managing any better.

She had some sort of answer the next afternoon, when she was interrupted in the middle of work by a messenger. He carried a long box containing one exquisite orchid. There was no card.

Lee contemplated the orchid at home that evening, wondering why she hadn't just picked up the phone and called Daniel. Even without a card the flower's perfection was a message in itself. Twice she put out her hand to the phone, but each time she pulled back.

The following afternoon she was in the middle of a stormy session with Roxanne when Gillian came over to interrupt.

'Not now,' Lee said impatiently.

'Lee, I think you'd better come.' Gillian's voice was urgent but she was struggling to hold back her laughter. 'There's been a special delivery.'

'Another orchid?'

'You could put it that way,' Gillian said cautiously.

At the door to her office Lee halted, unable to move further for the profusion of orchids. They covered everything, including the desk and chair. A large basketful stood on the floor by the far wall and another one blocked the entrance. Lee had to squeeze past it to get to the phone. Daniel answered so quickly that she knew he'd been sitting there, waiting for it to ring.

'You great clown,' she said tenderly.

'I thought you'd call me yesterday. When you didn't, I was sure you'd never forgive me.'

'There was no card. It might not have been you.'

'Who else sends you flowers? Tell me his name. I'll kill him!'

She joined in his laughter, but through the joking she could sense his nervousness.

'I'm sorry,' he said at last. 'I shouldn't have lost my temper and said the things I did. Forgive me, darling, *please*.'

'Of course,' she said at once, feeling joy flood through her. It was as though the man she loved had gone away for a time, but now he'd come back to her and she remembered afresh all the things that made him indescribably dear.

'Can you come here tonight?' he pleaded. 'I want to see you as soon as possible.'

'I'll come as soon as I've finished,' she said eagerly.

Everything was forgotten, including the sad and bitter thoughts that had tormented her. She hardly knew how she got through the rest of her work, but at last she was out of the door, hurrying to her car, her heart beating with anticipation as she threaded her way through the streets to Daniel's house.

The last time she'd come here he'd watched for her and opened the door, ready to do battle. Now it happened again, but this time everything was different. There was no anger in his eyes, but something else that stopped her heart. As soon as he'd pulled her inside his arms were around her, his lips on hers, and nothing else existed.

'Tell me everything's all right,' he begged. 'Say that you still love me.'

'Yes—yes—' The words became lost.

He kissed her with irresistible force, crushing her against him in an enveloping embrace. She kissed him back, swept by the need to reassure herself that he was still there, still Daniel, still hers.

'Never frighten me like that again,' he growled against her mouth, and immediately the pressure of his lips cut off her reply.

They clung to each other as if they'd been apart for years, as in a way they had. Their estrangement had been a great chasm across which they hadn't yet fully passed. The first quarrel had been a bitter shock to them both, and they were asking anxious questions about how they'd survived. The problems still lay in waiting for them, like rocks beneath the water, but for the moment they wouldn't think of them.

It was hard to remember that she'd ever been the unhappy woman of the last few days, the woman who'd pretended that she was still safe. Daniel's words, 'there's no safe place in love', came hazily back to her. She'd tried to love him without leaving her safe place and discovered that it wasn't possible. She tightened her arms round him and felt his answering embrace.

'It's all right,' he murmured. 'I'm here.'

'I'm so glad,' she said softly. 'Everything's all right if you're here.'

'Everything's all right,' he repeated. 'We're back together. We've had our first and last quarrel. It's over now and it'll never happen again.'

'No,' she said, holding him. 'It'll never happen again.'

He swept her up into his arms and began to mount the stairs. 'No more words, woman,' he growled in mock caveman style.

'Suppose Phoebe—?'

'She's out with your brother. I loaned him my car for the evening.'

'You shameless manipulator.'

'Yes, aren't I?' he said against her mouth. 'Now I don't want to think about either of them for a long time.' He kicked the door of the bedroom closed and laid her down gently on the bed. 'Lee, my darling...'

They undressed and fell onto the bed, seeking each other urgently, eager to find that the love which had always been so perfect before was a magic talisman to make trouble disappear.

At first it almost seemed as though they might succeed. The passion was there, undimmed, that fever in the flesh that briefly blotted out all else. Daniel made love to her more tenderly than ever before, whispering his love and need as he kissed her repeatedly. Yet gradually she sensed that something was still wrong. They were repeating the caresses and words of other lovings with a kind of ritual intensity, as though trying to recall memories. As though they were afraid of the here and now.

At the moment of greatest passion, the moment when their union had always been most complete and beautiful, she looked into his face and saw something like desperation, as though he would force everything to be right between them by sheer effort of will. Yet it couldn't be done, and they both knew it. The crack had been papered over but not mended.

Afterwards, as the pounding of her heart subsided, she lay in his arms, clinging to him tightly, not wanting to face the truth. They'd come back together because it was too painful to be apart, but their differences could still drive them asunder.

For now, they could pretend. They could speak in normal voices, laugh and kiss and carry on their lives, hoping that, with care, the fracture wouldn't grow larger. And if they didn't look too deeply into each other's eyes they might not see their mutual fear reflected.

At last Daniel sighed and said, 'There's nothing I can do about Phoebe, is there? We had another row today. I put my foot down but it simply went through the floor, so to speak. She's determined to defy me.

But it's not your fault,' he added quickly. 'I must have gone wrong somewhere.'

'She's not defying you because you went wrong,' Lee explained gently. 'She's defying you because you're trying to stop her pursuing her heart's desire. You can't do that, and you shouldn't want to. But you can stop her leaving home.'

'Not now she's sixteen and can earn her way,' he said in a brooding voice. 'She had the law about that at her fingertips.'

'Daniel, forget about the law. I mean you must stop her *wanting* to leave home. Don't drive her out with hostility. Be friendly and understanding—'

'You mean put up with it and smile? Pretend it's all right when it isn't?'

'Yes, that's just what I mean. It's part of being a parent, especially when your child has achieved independence. If you make the wrong move now you could lose her for life.'

He groaned. 'I suppose you're right, but how do you know all this? Sonya isn't old enough for you to be talking from experience.'

'In one way she is. Whenever she goes to visit Jimmy I have to fight the temptation to plead, "Don't believe anything he tells you". I plan excuses why she can't go, because I'm afraid she might not come back.'

'And do you ever actually try to stop her?'

'Never. And she always comes back. Sooner or later there's a point when the only way you can keep your children is to open your hands and set them free.'

'It might not be so bad,' he conceded reluctantly,

'if she goes on living here—and when she's working for you, you can keep an eye on her.'

'Yes, but Daniel—'

'You know who all the bad apples are, too—I mean the photographers that a young girl ought to avoid. You could tell this agency not to get her jobs with them.'

'I won't need to. It's a good agency. They'll protect her.'

'But if you tell them to assign her exclusively to you—'

'I thought you didn't want her working for me?'

'That's all changed,' he said impatiently. 'Yes, now I see how it can be—'

'Daniel, stop this!' Lee said firmly. 'You're doing it again.'

'Doing what?'

'Arranging Phoebe's life—and organising my professional diary as well. Darling, you can't do that. I'll use Phoebe if she's right for what I need, and if she isn't, I won't. And I certainly won't be telling Mulroy & Collitt what to do with their own client. The best way to protect Phoebe is for you to be nice to her so that she comes home to you every night. Make sure she knows you're always there for her. And then let go and *shut up*!'

He glared at her in displeasure. But at last a reluctant grin broke over his face. 'Maybe I'm being unnecessarily gloomy,' he conceded. 'How many new models try to break in every year?'

'Hundreds,' Lee said.

'And how many hit the big time?'

'One or two.'

'So with any luck she'll get just a few bookings and the whole thing will trickle to a halt.'

'So you're hoping for her to fail?' Lee said indignantly. 'That's nice, isn't it? How would Phoebe feel if she knew?'

'Darling, you won't tell her, will you?' he asked anxiously.

'No, I won't tell her. But I'm not going to do anything to blight her career, either, so don't even ask.'

'I wouldn't dream of it.' Daniel was becoming more cheerful, with his old conviction that the world would dance to his tune. 'Just—let things take their course and hope it all fades away.'

At ten o'clock he insisted he must watch the news, and they came downstairs. The next season of his TV show was due to start soon, so it made sense for him to keep abreast of current affairs, but Lee noticed the way he glanced at the clock at five-minute intervals.

'It's early yet,' she said encouragingly. 'My parents hit the roof if I stayed out until ten, but today's youngsters think nothing of it.'

'Do you mean Phoebe?' he asked casually. 'I hadn't given her a thought.'

Liar, Lee thought tenderly. *Oh, darling, you're such a rotten actor.*

Ten-thirty! Eleven! No sign of Phoebe. Daniel caught Lee glancing at the clock-face.

'It's much too soon for you to go home,' he said desperately. 'I'm just making some coffee.'

'Don't worry,' she soothed him. 'I'll stay with you until she comes in.'

'I don't know why you persist in thinking I'm worried. Phoebe's an independent young woman now. *Where the hell is she?*'

'With Mark,' Lee reminded him. 'He wouldn't let any harm come to her.'

There was a sound outside the front door. The two inside held their breath, trying to hear the softly murmuring voices. Then a key turned in the lock. Lee and Daniel went out into the hall to find Phoebe there with Mark. She looked at her father with an expression made up of defiance and appeal. Lee crossed her fingers, hoping Daniel wouldn't make a fatal mistake now.

For a moment the tension in the air was palpable. Then Daniel crossed the floor in two quick strides and enfolded his daughter in his arms. She hugged him back in passionate relief.

'I'm sorry about all those terrible things I said,' she whispered. 'I didn't mean them.'

'I didn't mean what I said, either,' Daniel told her in a ragged voice. 'But I haven't changed my position, darling.'

Phoebe raised her head from his shoulder and gave him a straight look. 'Nor have I, Daddy. It's my life and I'm going to do what *I* want to do with it.'

'Let's talk about that later—' he began.

'Yes, we'll have a nice long talk. I want you to understand why this is so important to me, and why I'm going to do it even if it means making you cross.'

His lips tightened a fraction. Lee held her breath.

'I thought you might have started to see sense—' he began.

Phoebe stepped back abruptly until she was standing beside Mark. Their fingers entwined. 'Daddy, if living here is just going to mean being hassled—'

It was as if red warning signs had lit up all around, telling Daniel that he was on the edge of the abyss.

'It isn't,' he said hastily. 'You've had your say and I've had mine.' Even at this moment a gleam of almost amused understanding passed between father and daughter, giving Lee a glimpse of the bitter quarrel they were now trying to bury. 'We'll just have to agree to differ. I want you safe at home. If I can't be happy about what you're doing, I can still promise no aggro.'

When she still hesitated a note of desperation came into his voice. 'This is very hard for me, Phoebe, but I'm trying. Don't make it more painful by going away. I'll lose you soon enough as it is, but I couldn't face a sharp break now. You can do this last thing for your poor old dad, can't you?'

A faint smile touched Phoebe's perfect mouth. As Lee had guessed, an appeal to the heart had swayed her where reasoning would have failed. She disentangled her fingers from Mark's and returned to Daniel, looking intently into his face. 'You promise not to nag and criticise me?'

'When have I ever—? I promise, I promise.'

'No sitting up to wait for me?'

'I can't promise that, but I won't make a big deal of it.'

'No interrogations?'

'No interrogations. But am I allowed to ask questions about your new life, out of curiosity?'

'Of course. But no pressure.'

'No pressure. I know you'll be sensible and not accept bookings that are a bit—you know…'

'A bit what?'

'You know,' he floundered. 'Posing in skimpy clothes with men who aren't wearing much either…'

'You mean underwear?' Phoebe asked, scandalised. 'I'm not going to model underwear. I'd die rather.'

'That's fine, darling, I'm glad you've got a sense of modesty and—'

'Brenda says that kind of work is a dead end,' Phoebe interrupted him earnestly. 'I'm going to the top, Dad, and you don't go to the top by modelling knickers and vests.'

They were still poles apart, but Daniel was fast learning the lesson of resignation and said meekly, 'I'll keep my opinions to myself in future. Besides,' he added with a wry touch of humour, 'if you're going to make a fortune, I may need to touch you for a hand-out.'

Phoebe's laughter pealed out and she hugged him fiercely. In her young, egotistical delight, she enjoyed her victory without conscience, unaware that her defeated opponent was hanging on the ropes. Only Lee saw the strain and sadness in Daniel's face before he bent to kiss his child.

Brenda Mulroy did her best to ease Lee's plight, inviting Daniel to her office and talking to him in a down-to-earth way about his daughter's prospects. She painted a realistic portrait of Phoebe's future career, which included the fact that several well-known photographers had already seen her pictures and been impressed. She meant to reassure him, but Lee knew that every encouraging word twisted a knife in his heart.

What reassured him more was Brenda herself, a plump, motherly woman in her fifties with a ready laugh. Even so, it took a while for his bristling defensiveness to subside, and that evening it all returned in a wave of black gloom.

'What about this course Phoebe's started?' he demanded of Lee as they stood in his kitchen watching a pot simmer.

'She needs to learn the tricks of the trade. The course will teach her what make-up to use and how to apply it for the camera. She'll learn things about her hair, her diet, her skin type, how to take care of herself—how to be a professional.'

'It sounds expensive.'

'A couple of thousand.'

'I knew it!' he said, outraged. 'It's nothing but a con trick to delude innocent girls into parting with their money.'

'Nonsense! Phoebe will pay it back out of her future earnings over the next year. I promise you, she'll earn a great deal more than two thousand. Please, Daniel, stop being paranoid.'

'Paranoid?' he growled. 'Of course I'm paranoid. I'm the father of a sixteen-year-old girl. It goes with the territory.'

Phoebe herself was blissfully happy, lost in graphs and colour charts, experimenting with a wide new range of products and techniques. She'd arrived home an hour earlier, greeted them cheerfully and hurried up to her room. When Daniel called that the meal was ready she descended with her face covered in green paste.

'It's a face mask,' she explained to her stunned father. 'I have to keep it on for a couple of hours.'

Daniel swallowed. 'Sit down at the table,' he said faintly.

Something was troubling Lee. 'Phoebe, weren't you supposed to be—?' The ringing of the front doorbell interrupted her.

Daniel answered it, and a moment later ushered Mark into the room. He was formally dressed and had started to say 'Is Phoebe ready yet—?' when he saw the green apparition and blenched. Phoebe's hands flew to her mouth.

'Oh, Mark, I'm so sorry. I forgot.'

'Forgot? After all the trouble I took to get the tickets—you forgot? Well, never mind. If you hurry we'll just make it.'

'But I can't take this off,' Phoebe said with a little scream. 'I've only just put it on.'

'Can't you put it on again when you come home?' Mark demanded in outrage.

'No, I've only got this one pot. Tomorrow I have to tell my instructor how it affected me.'

Mark tore his hair. 'The curtain goes up in an hour. Are you coming or not?'

'How can I come like this?' Phoebe protested.

'Well, what did you put it on for, woman?'

Daniel bristled at this form of address but Lee put a hand on his arm. 'I'm sure Phoebe can cope with Mark,' she murmured, 'Remember whose daughter she is.'

'I'm sorry,' Phoebe wailed. 'It just slipped my mind that we were going out tonight.'

'Oh, that's nice!' Mark exclaimed with heavy sarcasm. 'That's nice, isn't it? I may as well go, then.'

'You're welcome to stay and eat with us,' Daniel said.

'Thanks, but no thanks,' Mark said shortly. His handsome young face was marred by a petulant scowl. 'I won't stay where I'm not wanted.'

'You are wanted,' Lee pointed out. 'You've just been invited.'

'Some people don't want me,' Mark said with a black look at Phoebe. '*Some* people let me queue for tickets for the hottest show in town and then let it slip their mind. *Some* people forget me as soon as they have other interests and will probably be glad to see the back of me. Goodnight, everybody.'

'Stay for supper.' Lee repeated Daniel's invitation.

He threw her a smouldering look. 'Please don't worry about me. I can have a cheese sandwich when I get home.'

He departed with dignity. Lee struggled to control her face and even Daniel had to stop his lips twitching. Only Phoebe didn't find Mark's behaviour amusing. She gave a wail and flapped her hands.

'Don't worry too much,' Lee told her. 'It'll do him a power of good to know that your world doesn't revolve around him.'

'But I can't just let him go like that,' Phoebe wept, 'all hurt and miserable. Oh, how could I forget about tonight?'

'Because you had more important things to consider,' Daniel said with elaborate casualness. 'The trouble is, men resent women who are more successful than they are. Ouch! That was my shin.'

'Serves you right for saying something so prehistoric,' Lee hissed. 'You ought to be ashamed of trying to manipulate this situation.'

'I'm not. I just want to be sure Phoebe understands what's happening. Let him go, Phoebe. Be strong. Remember whose daughter you are.'

'I think you're hateful and heartless,' Phoebe cried. The next moment she was flying out into the street, calling, 'Mark, darling, wait—*please*.'

Daniel groaned. 'There's a sight that'll give the neighbours something to talk about for a week.'

Lee hardly heard him. For a moment the ghost of her young self was there, hurrying after Jimmy, begging him. 'Don't be angry, please, Jimmy... I didn't mean it... It was my fault...' To be eternally placating: the worst mistake you could make. Asking to be bullied.

'Anything wrong?' Daniel asked her.

'No,' she said hastily, and forced a smile to her face. 'Everything's fine.'

The young couple returned a few minutes later, apparently reconciled, but the rest of the evening wasn't a success. Phoebe refused to remove her face mask and Mark endured the meal with an air of gloom suitable to a man whose beloved had turned into Frankenstein's monster. Even when she finally washed her face matters were little improved, as she almost immediately announced her intention of going to bed.

'My instructor says I need early nights,' she said.

As the phrase 'my instructor says' had peppered the

conversation for the last two hours Lee felt that Mark could be forgiven for grinding his teeth. Daniel became notably more cheerful. Lee's brother had never been his favourite person, and his hostility had increased after the night Phoebe had taken his hand as a gesture of defiance. Mark had come to symbolise the malign fate that was distancing Phoebe from her father.

'What are you smiling at?' Lee demanded as they did the washing up.

'It's dawned on me that there may be an up side to this, after all. Think of the young men Phoebe will meet—young men with proper cars and not hoary old bangers. Men who know how to cherish a lovely girl and don't throw a fit of the sulks.'

'I think Mark was entitled to feel a little peeved,' Lee said indignantly. 'It took him ages to get those tickets, just to please her, and she simply forgot.'

'Nonetheless, it wasn't clever of him to descend into a self-pitying sulk.'

'So what should he have done, according to you?'

'Endured it with an air of noble suffering,' Daniel said with a wicked grin. 'Tossed the tickets away. What use are they if they don't please his lady? And if he could have contrived to suggest a broken heart bravely concealed beneath a casual air he'd have done himself a lot more good than he actually did.'

'That's what you'd have done, I suppose? In fact you've probably done just that at some time.'

'Well, the ladies I used to escort didn't usually forget,' Daniel admitted, with an air of false modesty that didn't fool her. 'But if they had, I'd have handled it better than that. I think I may just remind Phoebe how undignified he looked.'

Lee chuckled. 'You're a devious so-and-so. You're doing it again—arranging the world and everyone in it.'

'Don't you dare say I arrange things. I'm the helpless victim of events. But if Phoebe's career does bring this little romance to an end I shan't be sorry.' He glanced at the door, and finding that they were safely alone, sneaked a kiss. 'Do you have to go back early?' he murmured.

'Sonya's staying the night with a friend.'

'Thank heavens!'

'But I'm going home, Daniel. I know Phoebe's a modern girl, but—'

'I know,' he sighed. 'I feel the same. There's only one answer. You'll have to marry me.'

'We've got a lot of things to get out of the way first,' she prevaricated.

He searched her face and read in it everything she dared not say. Their reconciliation was fragile. Beneath the jokes and the affection they had retreated a little from each other. Who knew when they would recover the lost ground? Or whether it would ever be recovered?

She drove home and found Mark sitting in the kitchen, staring at a cup of cocoa. Lee patted his shoulder kindly. He really had been badly treated.

'Fifty quid those tickets cost me,' he muttered. 'Fifty flaming quid. And I had to queue in the rain. But what does she care?'

'Phoebe's very young, Mark,' Lee said sympathetically. 'At her age she doesn't want to get too serious.'

'That's not what she— Oh, hell, never mind!'

'You mean she made you think she was ready for a deep relationship?'

Mark shrugged disconsolately.

'But that was before her horizons broadened, wasn't it? Things are bound to change, my dear.'

'Yes, I'm just going to be a student to her, aren't I?'

'I don't think it's fair to ask any sort of commitment from her. Phoebe needs time to find her feet.'

'But I think about her all the time. You can't understand, Lee.'

'Can't I?' she asked, smiling a little at the age-old accusation.

'I don't suppose you even remember what it was like to be my age.'

Eighteen, she thought. When she'd been eighteen she'd already thought of her life as effectively over.

'Yes, I remember,' she said. 'Too well.'

CHAPTER EIGHT

AT THE end of the month-long course the modelling school gave a reception at which the students had the chance to put themselves on display. There was a small fashion show, with clothes provided by aspiring designers from a nearby fashion college. The audience was made up mostly of proud parents and friends, but there was also a smattering of fashion editors and photographers, seeking new talent.

'There are more professionals here than I've ever seen before,' Lee commented.

'I bet it's because of Phoebe,' Sonya said. She lowered her voice dramatically. 'A ripple has gone round the fashion world, and no one wants to miss the debut of this new star.'

'That would be lovely, darling, but it's the wrong time of year for Santa Claus,' Lee said with a smile.

But it seemed that Sonya was right. A fellow photographer accosted Lee with the words, 'They say the big discovery is all down to you'.

'I beg your pardon?'

'Phoebe Raife. Everyone's talking about her. Mind you, Brenda's playing it cool. She's turned down a couple of jobs already because they "weren't quite right for Phoebe". So now the pack's out in force to see if the reality lives up to the expectation.'

The show began. As soon as Phoebe appeared Lee knew that she'd made good use of the course. This was a subtly different creature from the eager girl she'd photographed only a couple of months ago. She was still young and fresh, but she'd acquired poise. Lee could hear again the clear, arrogant young voice saying 'I'm going to the top' and she wondered how they'd ever imagined that this young woman could be told what to do.

Perhaps Daniel thought the same, for his eyes were fixed on his daughter with a kind of awe mixed with sadness.

Sonya was simply thrilled.

'Wasn't she wonderful?' she demanded afterwards. 'Like Phoebe and yet—not like Phoebe at all.'

'No,' Daniel said with a sigh. 'Not like Phoebe at all.'

Sonya looked at him with sympathy and slipped a comforting hand into his. Recently it had become common for her and Lee to dine with him, and for Sonya to retire to his study afterwards to do her homework. One evening Daniel took her in a cup of tea and remained away for nearly half an hour. Going to find him, Lee had discovered them earnestly discussing her history essay. Sonya's eyes had been bright with interest, and Daniel had seemed equally absorbed. After that they became firm friends, and she called him Daniel.

When the fashion show was over they drank champagne and waited for the models to reappear. Phoebe bounded over, an eager youngster again, and Daniel fixed an enthusiastic smile on his face by sheer effort of will.

'You were wonderful, darling,' he said.

'Did you really think so? You're not just—?'

'Wonderful,' he repeated firmly, determined to do the thing properly.

'Lee?' Phoebe turned to her in appeal.

'You made a sensation,' Lee told her truthfully. 'There's already a lot of interest in you.'

Phoebe gave a little delighted scream, then looked around the crowded room. 'Where's Mark?'

'He really wanted to come,' Lee said awkwardly. 'But now that term has started again... He's working on an essay that has to be in on Monday. He sent you his best wishes.'

Phoebe's face fell. 'Yes, of course,' she said bravely.

In fact Mark had sulkily refused to attend. He'd pleaded pressure of work, but he'd always been able to get out of that before when he wanted to, and of course Phoebe knew this. Mark was jealous, and it made him unkind.

There were a dozen people eager to claim Phoebe's attention. Sonya slipped away into a corner where she could take a sip of champagne in defiance of her mother's prohibition. Lee was left alone with Daniel, who was scowling.

'How dare he snub my daughter?' he said angrily.

'You should be glad. Phoebe can see for herself that he's being very immature, which is surely what you want.'

'Of course it's what I want. The sooner she gets over her infatuation with that high-handed young puppy the better.'

'Well, then—'

'But he's still got no right to snub my daughter and make her unhappy,' Daniel said stubbornly.

The following day Brenda accepted an assignment for Phoebe, and after that she was seldom out of work.

'It's almost laughable,' Lee complained to Gillian eventually. 'Daniel assumed I'd be keeping Phoebe in work, but I can hardly get her. I want her for that jeans ad. It's going to be a huge spread, and three days' work for the models, but Brenda ummed and ahhed for ages before letting me have one day as a special favour.'

A week later she encountered a situation that exasperated her even more.

'I can't believe it,' she fumed to Daniel. 'I just cannot...' Words failed her.

'Have a sherry,' he said soothingly, pressing her back into the leather cushions of his sofa. 'Calm down. Then tell me all about it.'

'I get a call from Lindsay Elwes, the fashion editor of *Woman Of The World*, which is a magazine I've always wanted to work for. It's not *Vogue* or *Tatler*, but it's coming up very fast. Lindsay wants me to take the pictures for a big wedding spread. Then we come to the crunch line. She desperately wants Phoebe to be one of the models but Brenda's not keen, because Phoebe's schedule is so tight. But *I'm* supposed to be able to get her because of my "personal connections". No Phoebe, no assignment.'

'It must be maddening for you, darling,' Daniel said, preserving a straight face.

'If you dare to laugh—'

'I'm not, I swear it,' he said in a shaking voice.

'It's not the only time—I mean, there have been hints before—but this is the first time an editor I really mind about has said it openly. After all the years I've been in this business, building up my credit, suddenly I'm just the door to Phoebe—a girl *I* started off. Did you say something?' she demanded ominously.

'I wouldn't dare. After all, what can I say except that if anyone has been hoist with her own petard—But I'm not saying that,' he added hastily, reading retribution in her eyes.

'Well, it's not fair,' she said crossly. 'I've really dreamed about that last step up. I want to be in demand in my own right, not...' She sighed.

'I guess it's not enough to take terrific pictures of fashionable people,' Daniel observed. 'You need to be fashionable yourself.'

'Oh, I'm fashionable all right,' Lee said crossly. 'As Phoebe Raife's friend.'

'She's doing well, isn't she?'

'She's a real success, and she's loving every minute of it. She was modelling jeans for me today. In fact, we had a bit of a chat.' She eyed him.

'Ah!' Daniel said uneasily.

'You're not really keeping all those promises you made her, are you?'

'I'm trying, Lee, I really am. But it's hard when I see her doing silly things. Take the food she eats—or doesn't eat. She's starving herself. Her figure's perfect, but because of this modelling nonsense she's obsessed with the fear of being fat.'

'She's not obsessed and she's not starving,' Lee explained patiently. 'She's trimmed off exactly five pounds, because the camera makes people look a little fatter. Now she's eating sensibly to maintain her new weight. She showed me her diet sheet and it's excellent—lots of low-fat, high-nourishment foods. She's full of energy.'

'So what would have been wrong with one little steak?'

'It was a big steak,' said Lee, who'd heard this story from Phoebe. 'And you fried it in butter and tried to make her eat it with chips. If you'd grilled it and cut out the chips she'd have eaten it.'

'She's always loved steak and chips. She used to say that no one cooked them like I did. But that seems a long time ago.'

The chasm yawned between them again. Looking across it, Lee saw blame in his eyes. 'She still loves steak and chips,' she said. 'That's why she refused them so vehemently. She was afraid she'd be tempted. It's not easy to turn down something you desperately want to eat. You should admire her strength of character.'

'Even when she's strong against me, you mean, don't you?'

'Well—'

'All right,' he broke in hastily, for he too had seen the danger. 'Let's drop it.'

'Not until I've given you your present,' Lee said, getting up.

'What present? It's not my birthday.'

She reached into the depths of her bag and pulled out a parcel. 'Open it,' she said.

Puzzled, he did so, and found himself looking at a book. *'The Low Fat Cookbook,'* he said, and a grin spread over his face. 'Clever. Very clever.'

'I bought that for you this afternoon when I left work. It's just what you need to get back into

Phoebe's good books. Ask her to give you a copy of her diet sheet. It'll tell you what she needs to eat and in what amounts. Then find the recipes that fit.

'And another thing. Presentation is important. You'll need to do a lot of checking to get the amounts right, so let her see you weighing food very precisely. And don't tell her this was my idea. *You* thought of it and scoured the shops until you found this book.'

'Did I?' He looked startled.

'Certainly you did. When she feels you're on her side things will come right between you again.'

He hugged her. 'Thank you, darling. I've been feeling completely cast adrift, but with your help I'll find the far shore.' He added wryly, 'Although what it will look like I can't imagine.'

'The important thing is that Phoebe will be there too.'

'And you?' he asked, suddenly intense. 'Will you be there?'

'Maybe. Who knows what the future holds?'

'Say yes, Lee. Marry me. I need you.'

'Don't press me, Daniel. Wait and see how things work out.'

He smiled and conceded, but a light had gone out inside him. Lee felt distracted. She loved Daniel, but she was further than ever from marrying him. Now every casual chat was a minefield. Their old, easy, happy association seemed only a memory. Love held them together—just—but the gap was always there, growing inexorably wider. How long would it be, she wondered, before it was too wide for them to reach across, or even to see each other?

* * *

A week later Daniel made a date with her, but beyond telling her to dress up to the nines—'And I really mean the nines.'—he refused even to hint at their destination. Lee called Carol Halden, a fashion editor she was friendly with, to ask advice. The result was the loan of a black slinky dress that brought out a *femme fatale* side she hadn't known she possessed.

'Wow!' Sonya said when she saw it. 'It really suits you, Mum.'

'Thank you, darling. Will you be all right here this evening?'

'Course I will. I won't be alone—unfortunately. My *uncle* will be here.'

'Why have you suddenly started calling Mark uncle? I know he *is*, but why suddenly now?'

'The other day he actually dared to say I ought to show him some respect. I ask you! Five years older than me, and he tries to come the heavy uncle.'

'So now you're making him regret he ever mentioned it?'

'Of course.' Sonya giggled. 'It makes him so mad.'

'I wish you two could get on better.'

'No one could get on with Mark in his present mood. He goes around looking mournful so that everyone knows his heart has been broken by a cruel goddess.'

'Has he finally broken up with Phoebe?'

'We-ell, hard to say if it's final. He saw her being driven by a young man in a Mercedes. Phoebe said he was only a photographer driving her to the location of a shoot.'

'How silly of Mark to make a fuss about it.'

'Apparently the car stopped at traffic lights and

Mark crossed in front and got a grandstand view of them laughing together. Phoebe looked up and there was Mark glowering at her through the windscreen, very much the student: jeans, trainers and a day's growth of beard. Of course, *she* looked as if she'd stepped out of a bandbox. Mark just stood there while the lights changed, and the man had to toot his horn to make him move.'

'Oh, dear,' Lee said sympathetically. 'At his age that kind of thing feels like a real tragedy.'

'They were supposed to have a date that night.'

'She didn't forget again, did she?'

'No, but she was late. It wasn't her fault. The shoot overran and the photographer actually drove her to meet Mark—in his Mercedes. Of course, Mark threw a wobbly. Now he's waiting for her to apologise. He's been waiting for a week.'

'How do you know all this? Don't tell me Mark confides in you?'

'Not exactly confides. He just moans incessantly while I'm in earshot. I wish he wouldn't. It's dead boring.'

'Poor Mark.'

'He'll survive,' Sonya said cheerfully.

It was probably for the best, Lee decided. At Mark's age romances came and went. Then she forgot about him in thinking ahead to the evening with Daniel.

He whistled when he saw her, and nodded in satisfaction. 'Just perfect for this,' he said, producing a long, flat box and raising the lid. Inside, a diamond pendant and matching earrings glittered against black velvet. Lee caught her breath.

Daniel fixed the pendant about her neck and the earrings to her ears, then turned her so that she could see herself in the mirror. She could hardly believe that the glamorous creature looking back was herself. This woman was poised, sophisticated, and she matched the man beside her, dressed in a dinner jacket and bow tie. She gave a little pleasurable shiver.

'Darling, I—'

He kissed her. 'Don't say anything. I'd like to spend my whole life giving you things.' Before she could reply he added, 'The taxi's here. No driving for me tonight. We're having gallons of champagne and I want to be able to enjoy it.'

The 'taxi' turned out to be a chauffeur-driven Rolls Royce. Lee began to feel as though she was moving in a dream.

'Where are we going?' Lee asked as the car moved off.

'Miranda's,' he replied simply.

Lee gasped. Miranda's was a nightclub that had opened a couple of months earlier and had fast acquired a reputation as *the* place to party. Being seen there was a sign that you were 'in'. Surely, Lee thought, Daniel was indifferent to that sort of trend? But maybe a television celebrity had to nod in its direction once in a while.

'Is it a special occasion?' she asked.

'Sort of. I've arranged a surprise for you.'

When they entered, heads turned at the sight of the famous Daniel Raife with a mystery companion. Everywhere she looked Lee saw well-known show business people. They all greeted Daniel and shook hands with Lee.

She noticed some friends—a model, a fashion editor, a photographer. They greeted her in her own right and this time it was *she* who made the introductions. She began to feel more at home, and by the time they sat down to eat she was at ease.

'Is this the surprise?' she asked as Daniel refilled her champagne glass.

'No, that's still to come. Wait and see.' He lifted his glass. 'Here's to you. And thank you.'

'For what?' she asked, clinking her glass against his.

'For the cookbook. It's a great success. Phoebe was thrilled that I was helping her.'

The next moment Jon Harriman, a gossip columnist, joined them. 'Daniel, introduce me,' he said jovially, his eyes flickering appraisingly over Lee.

'Lee, this is Jon Harriman, whose column you read avidly every day,' Daniel said.

'Do I? I mean, yes, of course I do.'

Harriman chuckled amiably. He was a big man with a jolly face, and Lee found herself liking him. Daniel completed the introductions.

'Jon, this is Lee Meredith, the well-known fashion photographer.'

To Lee's surprise Harriman instantly said, 'Loved that stuff you had in *Vogue* last month. I know all the fashion editors, and they speak highly of you.'

He mentioned other things she'd done, proving that he really did know her work. Lee couldn't help being flattered, and then she realised that this was a golden opportunity to raise her profile. With a little encouragement from Jon Harriman she began to talk about herself. He was a good listener, drawing her out and seeming to be really interested.

Daniel claimed her for a dance. The lights were low and the music sweet. As he held her close Lee wished they could always be like this, cocooned in their own world, with problems far away. Tonight she could forget the uneasiness that was always there, just below the surface of their relationship, and think only of the fact that she loved him. If only love alone could be enough.

She looked up and saw him watching her, his lips close to hers. He dropped a soft kiss on her mouth. There was a sudden flash of light and Lee blinked.

'Just one more,' said a man's voice, and when she looked he clicked the camera again.

'Do people always take your picture when you come to nightclubs?' she asked Daniel.

'Sometimes, which is why I hardly ever come.'

'But Daniel, that man—'

'Forget it,' he said, swinging her around until her head whirled. 'Let's dance, sweetheart. The night is young yet.'

She slept later than usual next morning and came downstairs in her dressing gown. She'd drunk only moderately at Miranda's, but it had been five a.m. before she slid into her bed, and her whole body was protesting that it needed to finish its sleep. Her eyes, in particular, didn't want to open, and she almost groped her way into the kitchen. Sonya guided her the rest of the way, sat her at the table and set a cup of tea in front of her.

'Thank you, darling, but shouldn't you be at school?'

'I'm just about to go. Besides, I wanted to be the one to show you the newspaper.'

'Why? What's happened?'

'Drink your tea first.'

She sipped the tea, finally managing to get her eyes to function. Sonya laid the paper out on the table, open at the gossip column. At the top was a picture of Jon Harriman beside the headline JON'S DAY 'N' NIGHT. Halfway down the page was a picture of herself and Daniel, dancing. Then, there was a piece of text.

> For the first time TV star Daniel Raife took the wraps off his new love, top fashion photographer Lee Meredith. They met when she took his picture for the cover of his latest book and have seen a lot of each other since. Last night they were at Miranda's, and although they wouldn't admit to being more than just good friends it was clear that neither had eyes for anyone else. Daniel refused to say much about the lady, but when I asked if we could expect an announcement soon he didn't throw me out. Any guesses what that means, folks? Lee works for all the top magazines, and is in great demand...

There was more, but before Lee could finish reading the phone rang. Sonya lifted the receiver off the kitchen wall, and Lee heard her say, 'Hi, Gillian. Yes, Mum's here, but she's not *compos mentis* yet. A bit of the morning-after-the-night-before—'

'Give me the phone while I have some reputation left,' Lee commanded, stretching out her hand. 'Hello, Gillian. Don't take any notice of that little wretch. I'm just half-asleep.'

'Have you seen the paper?' Gillian asked excitedly.

'This minute. I can't believe my eyes.'

'Jon Harriman has really done you proud, hasn't he? The phone hasn't stopped ringing this morning. Your diary's filling up fast. That's what I called to say. Everyone's curious about you.'

Lee woke up abruptly. 'People want me to take pictures because I was seen with Daniel in Miranda's? It doesn't make sense.'

'That's how celebrity works,' Gillian said cheerfully. 'You're as good as all the top names, and better than some, but they've been "in" and you've been "out". At least, not "out" exactly, but hovering on the fringes. Now you're "in".'

'I can't follow that when I've only just got up,' Lee complained.

'OK, finish waking up. Then come into work and enjoy your fame.'

Lee read the piece through. Jon Harriman had turned her into an overnight celebrity. Of course her fame would be fleeting, unless she made it last by building on it. Gillian was right. She was as good as the best, but they'd had fashionable contacts at work for them and she hadn't—until now.

She called Daniel and Phoebe answered. 'Dad's asleep,' she said. 'He left me a note saying he's not to be disturbed, but he'll call you at the studio later.'

She giggled. 'He also told me to find out what sort of mood you're in.'

'You can tell him grateful,' Lee said with a smile.

'I'm so excited,' Phoebe bubbled. 'You looked smashing in that dress.'

Lee's first act was to despatch the dress back to Carol Halden, the fashion editor who'd loaned it. She was on the phone to the studio within minutes of Lee's arrival.

'Aren't you a dark horse?' she drawled. 'Darling, he's the most exciting man in London. So when do we get the announcement?'

'You don't. We're just good friends.' As Lee said the traditional words she felt a blush go right through her body. Carol roared with laughter.

'All right, I'll wait patiently—or impatiently. Fancy you and Daniel Raife being a couple.'

'Yes,' Lee said slowly. 'Fancy.' It was dawning on her that perhaps there was more to this than met the eye.

She was sure of it later that evening, when Jimmy telephoned. He'd seen the paper. Sonya took the call and relayed her father's comments to Lee.

'Dad says he hopes Daniel Raife is loaded,' she said, 'because it would be a shame for you to miss out twice.'

'Tell your father, from me, not to be vulgar,' Lee retorted.

'Dad, Mum says don't be vulgar...Mum, he says it's too late now.'

'Don't you have homework to do?' Lee enquired frostily.

When Daniel called her his first words were, 'Are you mad at me?'

'For doing me a favour?' she asked lightly. 'Why should I be?'

'For showing you off to the world without asking you first.'

'No, I like it. Being known only as a rung on Phoebe Raife's ladder was undermining my self-confidence. After last night I can double my prices.'

'That's the spirit. And in a few years I'll be boasting that I once knew Lee Meredith—that is, if you still remember me by then.'

'Stop fishing,' she told him wryly. His self-confident chuckle was the last thing she heard before she put the phone down.

She sat musing for a while, recognising again what a very subtle operator Daniel was. Under cover of doing her a favour, he'd established them publicly as a couple—which meant he'd taken her a step further along the path to marriage than she'd meant to travel.

Lee had too much good sense to complain that she was famous for the wrong reason. Daniel, who knew the value of publicity, had done her a kindness and done it very thoroughly, and she was honestly grateful.

Just the same, he'd once more arranged matters the way he wanted them, and Lee couldn't help regarding her beloved somewhat wryly.

CHAPTER NINE

IT SEEMED there was no end to the little pinpricks that Phoebe's success could deliver to her father. For his birthday she blew a hole in her budget by buying him a winter coat of black leather. When he protested at the expense she said airily, 'It's all right, Daddy. I got it wholesale. Turn around again. I want to see how fabulous you look.'

Then she, Sonya and Lee applauded while he showed his pleasure by grinning self-consciously. It was a happy scene, but he would gladly have given it up if only Phoebe had been able to spend the day with him. Unluckily an important booking was taking her in one direction just as he was setting out for a family party in the other.

Lee and Sonya accompanied him to his old home in the Midlands, where his mother still lived in the comfort he provided for her. Jean and Sarah, his sisters, also turned up, leaving Lee in no doubt that she was being looked over as a future addition to the family.

She liked the Raife women, who were all tall, like Phoebe, although without her beauty. They had her sharp wits too. They greeted Lee warmly and with a kind of relief, as though she was the long-awaited answer to prayers. She wished she knew what Daniel had told them about her.

She was particularly drawn to Jean, the eldest of

the three siblings. At forty-three Jean was unmarried, stylish, and had a booming, abrupt voice that spared nobody, not even the brother she adored.

After lunch she showed Lee over the garden, which was only just losing its colour. 'What about this Phoebe business?' she demanded, coming straight to the point. 'Taking it hard, isn't he?'

'Very hard. He had his heart set on her going to Oxford.'

'Plenty of time for that later. Girls of sixteen don't yearn for the life of the mind.'

'But—didn't you?'

Jean roared with laughter. 'He tell you that? Well, of course I wanted to finish my education, and I minded that my father was a blithering idiot about it. But it wasn't the whole of life. Secretly I yearned to be drop-dead gorgeous and have men prostrating themselves at my feet—especially Jack Denis.'

'Who was Jack Denis?'

'Local heart-throb. My, he was handsome! An Adonis. Pity he was as thick as a plank.'

'Didn't he notice you?' Lee asked sympathetically.

'Not him. He married the daughter of a pig farmer. Now the place is theirs. She does the paperwork and he looks after the porkers—although I think he finds even that a bit mentally challenging.' She joined in Lee's laughter.

'If I'd had Phoebe's beauty I'd have wanted to make the most of it, not have my father droning on that there were more important things in life.'

'Yes, there's a lot Daniel doesn't understand.'

'My little brother is a very brilliant man—in his way,' Jean said drily. 'But when it comes to coping with a daughter about to leave the nest he's as big a fool as the rest of the male sex. He told me about the steak and chips fiasco. Luckily for him a first-class mind came to the rescue with some low-fat cooking.'

'Hey,' Lee said indignantly, '*I* bought him that book.'

'Did I say otherwise?'

'You said a first-class mind.'

'I meant yours. A mind that can see straight to the heart of the problem and pinpoint the answer. You did that while he was still floundering.'

'That's the first time anyone's praised my mind,' Lee mused.

'Sonya has a good brain too. Gets it from you. Daniel won't go far wrong while he's got you to put him straight.'

'I'm not so sure,' Lee said sadly. 'He copes on the surface, but underneath he's tense and miserable. I can't reach him. In his heart I think he still blames me.'

'A man has to blame somebody—as long as it isn't himself.'

'But things used to be so perfect between us.'

'Sure about that?' Jean asked shrewdly.

'I beg your pardon?'

'In my experience nothing is ever perfect. It just looks that way afterwards. Love is very difficult. That's why I never tried it after I got over the pigman. Why make it even harder by longing for an impossible ideal? It wastes what you could have now. And what you and Daniel could have is very special.'

While Lee was trying to decide how to respond Jean said briskly, 'I've enjoyed our talk. I'm sure you're just the woman Daniel needs to keep him in order.'

'Thank you,' Lee said, without much conviction.

Lee normally breakfasted off coffee and toast, but on the day of the big wedding dress shoot for *Woman Of The World* she made herself bacon and eggs and plenty of it.

'That's not like you,' Mark observed.

'I've got a very tough day ahead,' she told him. 'Five models, two make-up experts, two hairdressers, one fashion editor and twenty wedding garments. I'm going to need all my strength.'

'Oh, yes,' he said, elaborately casual. 'You've mentioned this wedding shoot.'

'More than once, probably,' Lee admitted. 'I was so furious that they only wanted me because of Phoebe. Ah, well, I got her so it all worked out well in the end. Bye, folks. Sonya, don't be late for school.'

She reached the studio to find Gillian just ahead of her, and a moment later a van full of clothes arrived. Lindsay Elwes, the fashion editor, burst in, full of agitation.

'I'm already on my first nervous breakdown of the day,' she confessed. 'Stephanie's let me down. Flu or something. I've been on to the model agencies but there's nobody suitable available, so I've got to re-write the roster to divide Steph's dresses amongst the others.'

'Don't worry,' Lee soothed her. 'It'll all work out. It always does.'

'Aren't any of them here yet?' Lindsay demanded in a suppressed shriek.

'Yes. Roxanne's just walking through the door now, and Phoebe's right behind her.'

The mention of Phoebe's name brought a smile to Lindsay's face. 'Isn't she divine?' she murmured. 'Lee, you're so clever to have got her for me.'

She wafted away to embrace the models. Within the next five minutes everyone who was missing turned up, and a kind of peace descended. Lee and Lindsay discussed the order of the shots while the models got dressed and started working on their looks.

The idea was to demonstrate a wide range of wedding clothes from the simple to the flamboyant, from the traditional to the ultra-modern. Phoebe had been assigned the outfits designed for very young brides. Her first one was a trouser suit made of ivory wild silk. On her head she wore a wide-brimmed hat modelled on the *borsalino* headgear favoured by gangsters in old Hollywood films, except that it, too, was of ivory silk. The idea was outrageous, but Phoebe made it work. On her graceful frame the outfit became cheeky, ingenious and fun.

Her next costume was a skintight body stocking in white stretch satin, over which were draped a couple of silk chiffon scarves. One huge flower was perched aslant on her head. Lee shot her with Roxanne, who was dressed as a shepherdess, with panniers and a basket full of flowers. The contrast between the two was breathtaking.

Lindsay Elwes performed miracles of organisation in distributing the absent Stephanie's dresses among the other models. At last she was left with only one garment that hadn't been reassigned.

'Roxanne, I think...' she murmured.

'Roxanne won't have time to get changed after the last tableau,' Lee objected.

'That's right, she won't. And Julia will just be putting on that Victorian thing—it'll have to be Phoebe.'

'I thought you wanted to keep her for the young, modern stuff.'

'Yes, I did,' Lindsay sighed. 'But there's no choice. She's the only one with the time to do it.'

The dress was made of silk chiffon and swept the ground. It was cut on classical lines, without even a hint of decoration. Even the floor-length veil was unadorned, held in place by two small pearls. Lee had her doubts about Phoebe in this conservative style, until she actually saw the girl wearing it. Then she drew in her breath.

Phoebe's blazing beauty was accentuated by the gown's simple lines. With her head slightly bent, a bouquet of lilies in her hand, she looked the essence of gentle femininity and grace.

Lee photographed her with the others in ones and twos, then by herself. 'Take some more of her alone,' Lindsay muttered, and Lee nodded. Already she could see that this was going to be *the* shot of the spread.

'Twirl,' she instructed Phoebe, who did so. The glorious gown and veil swirled out about her in a soft cloud.

After a few more minutes she called, 'OK, that's it!'

She'd half noticed a new presence in the studio. Now she turned to look and saw that it was Mark.

She gave him a friendly greeting. 'How long have you been there?'

He didn't answer. His gaze was riveted on Phoebe and his mouth had fallen open. She seemed to become aware of him and a slow smile spread over her face. Lee understood that smile. It was triumph that she'd brought her lover back to her feet, but it was innocent of any malice. Phoebe was simply enjoying her newly discovered power as a woman.

She walked slowly across the studio, stopped a precisely judged distance away from Mark and sank into a deep curtsey. The gorgeous dress flared out around her, as she'd known it would. She looked utterly entrancing, and Lee swiftly raised her camera again, praying that Phoebe wouldn't move until she had the picture. And of course Phoebe didn't.

'Do you like me?' she asked impishly of Mark.

He made a sound like a man being strangled. 'You—you look—' he stammered. 'You look just—just—'

'Phoebe, I need that dress,' Lindsay called, and Phoebe wafted away, with a slight backward glance at Mark. He gazed after her, rooted to the spot.

'Mark!' Lee waved a hand in front of his face. 'Come back to earth.'

'I didn't know,' he breathed. 'I never dreamed...'

'She's quite something, isn't she?'

'Quite something? Is that any way to talk about her? She's a goddess—Venus rising from the waves—the face that launched a thousand ships. She's Helen of Troy for whom men died. She's—'

'All right, I get your drift,' Lee said kindly. 'Come and have some coffee and sandwiches with me.'

'I couldn't eat,' he protested in a daze.

'Just honey and nectar, huh?'

'What?'

'Never mind.' She patted his hand. 'Enjoy it while you're young.'

'All my life,' he murmured. 'All my life.'

'I thought you were never going to speak to her again.'

'That was before I knew,' he said simply.

Phoebe reappeared wearing her street clothes, but it was obvious that to Mark she still carried the aura that had surrounded her in the wedding gown.

'I've got the car outside,' he said. Phoebe laid her hand in his without a word and they left the studio together.

After that the atmosphere in Lee's home improved dramatically. Whatever had happened between Mark and Phoebe, his shining happiness confirmed that the reconciliation was complete.

'He helped me with my maths homework last night,' Sonya told Lee one day, adding with a giggle, 'Mind you, his mind's in such a whirl that I checked it carefully afterwards.'

'Did he tell you anything about how things are going? I don't like to ask him myself in case I'm accused of nagging.'

'The path of true love isn't entirely smooth,' Sonya said dramatically. 'Our hero's noble soul still has much to suffer.'

'Such as?'

'I think he's going to talk to you about his car.'

'Oh, heavens! Not again!'

'No, he's going to take the three thousand. He

knows you're not going to let him have seven, and he really can't keep taking Phoebe out in that tomato on wheels. So he's going to give in without actually admitting that he's giving in. You'll be careful what you say to him, won't you, Mum?'

'I'll try to be tactful, darling,' Lee said meekly.

'He's madly sensitive about money, now Phoebe's earning so much. He took her to dinner last week and she lacerated his feelings by offering to go Dutch. Luckily she saw the light in time and meekly allowed him to pay for her.'

'Daniel Raife's daughter did that?'

'She's in love,' Sonya intoned, in the manner of someone announcing a terminal disease. 'And so is he. Honestly, they're dead boring, both of them. What's that for, Mum?' Lee had given her an impulsive hug.

'It's gratitude, darling. At least one person around here has kept a clear head on her shoulders.'

'You wait till it's my turn,' Sonya said wickedly. 'Any day now I'm due to turn into a fiend who stays out late every night, wears punk make-up, dates yobbos and snarls, "Gerroff my back!" every time you speak to me. Most girls my age are already doing that, but luckily for you I'm a late developer.'

'Thank you, darling,' Lee said faintly.

In fact her relationship with Sonya was fast becoming the one stable point in a turbulent world. Mark's moods were on a roller coaster, depending on how often he saw Phoebe.

The negotiations about the car money were handled delicately on both sides. Mark loftily deigned to accept three thousand pounds, without any reference to their previous battles. What Sonya had called 'the tomato on wheels' vanished, never to be seen again, and its place was taken by a silver-blue saloon.

For a while peace reigned, but the next upset was just over the horizon. And the cause, as Sonya had hinted, was Mark's sensitivity about money.

Lee came downstairs one morning with a headache. She'd slept badly, as she often did these days, and felt far from ready for the day. She collected the mail and began to sort sleepily through it. There were bills for herself and something for Mark that she recognised as his credit card statement. It was a source of friction between them as whenever he had trouble meeting the monthly payment, which was usually, he nagged her to increase his allowance. Lee always refused and advised him to economise, which annoyed him.

'Give this to Mark, please,' she said to Sonya, who was just coming downstairs.

Lee went into her den to open her mail. While she was frowning over an invoice she was startled to hear Sonya's voice reach her from the kitchen across the hall.

'Mum will go absolutely ballistic when she sees that.'

Then Mark's voice. 'She isn't going to see it. Anyway, no woman tells me what to do.'

Lee hurried out and reached the kitchen door just as Sonya said, 'Don't be a prat, Mark. Of course she'll find out.'

'Find out what?' Lee asked. The two of them jumped. In the silence Lee looked from one to the other. Sonya's lips were firmly pressed together and

Mark wore an uncomfortable look, at variance with his defiant words.

The credit card statement lay open on the table. An instinct for trouble made Lee glance at it.

'Two thousand pounds!' she exclaimed, aghast. 'Since when was your credit limit that high?'

'I only just increased it,' Mark said sulkily.

'You had no right to. One thousand is more than enough.'

'Oh, stop making a fuss! I haven't actually used up the two thousand. It's just there—in case I need it.'

'This is because of Phoebe, isn't it?'

'You know what she's earning. How can I entertain her on a student's grant?'

'And you think the answer is to run up debt in the hope that I'll hand over your inheritance?'

'It's about time you did,' he shouted.

'Acting like this isn't going to persuade me that you're responsible about money.'

'It's my money!'

'Not until you grow up.' She became aware of Sonya watching with bright-eyed eagerness and said briefly, 'Scram!'

When Lee and Mark were alone she spoke more gently. 'You've got it really badly, haven't you?'

He gave a mirthless laugh. 'That's putting it mildly. That day in the studio, when I saw her in the wedding dress—I've never seen anything so beautiful in my life. She looked like an angel. I'm in love with her. She's the only girl I'll ever love.'

Oh, the delusions of youth! Lee regarded him sympathetically. 'But this isn't the way, my dear,' she said kindly. 'If Phoebe were the kind of girl who only cares about a man's money—well, you wouldn't be able to compete. But I don't think she's like that. Does she tell you how she feels about you?'

'Oh, yes, she says she loves me,' he replied wretchedly.

'Then can't you trust her?'

'I do trust her, but I get scared. If you'd only see sense, Lee, and hand over the cash—'

'No,' she said, her eyes kindling. 'It's there to safeguard your future. I'd be crazy to let you blow it on your first infatuation.'

'I'm nineteen now. That's old enough to have what's mine.'

'Not according to your trust.'

'The hell with the trust!'

Lee's headache had grown worse. If only Mark would stop this. 'Is there any tea in the pot?' she asked, turning away.

'Never mind that now. It's time we had this out.' Mark took hold of her arm and pulled her around to face him.

Lee's temper flared and she shook herself free. 'Stop trying to bully me. As far as I'm concerned we've already had it out—too often. The money stays where it is until you're older, and that's my last word on the subject.'

'Well, it's not *my* last word on the subject. Don't think you're going to get away with this.'

'Oh, Mark, please! Stop talking like a character in a bad melodrama. It doesn't move me, except to make me want to laugh.'

CHAPTER TEN

LEE told the whole story to Daniel that night as she nestled against him on the sofa.

'I don't know why I accuse you of handling Phoebe badly,' she sighed. 'I'm making a complete hash of it with Mark. Does Phoebe storm out of the front door?'

'Not her. It might disarrange her hair. She's a smart cookie, my Phoebe.'

'That's the first compliment I've heard you pay her since this started.'

'Yes, well...' He looked awkward and changed the subject. 'Some more wine?'

'Just a tiny drop. Do you know, if it wasn't so early I'd swear I heard Mark's car stopping outside.'

'It is,' he said, alert. 'It's got a distinctive sound and I should know it by now—the nights I've stood at the window listening for it!'

'I hope you don't let Phoebe know that.'

He grinned. 'Don't worry. I know better than to put myself forward, these days.' He slid an arm around Lee. 'I guess I've learned the lesson you tried to teach me.'

'What's that?'

'That you have to let go to hold on.' A hint of self-mockery crept into his tone. 'You wouldn't recognise me. I creep about the house in fear and trembling, and if Phoebe speaks to me I stand to attention. If she can spare me ten minutes from her busy schedule I'm properly grateful. I've even learned the difference between acceptable interest and unforgivable intrusion.'

'Tell me! Tell me! I might manage better with Mark.'

'Acceptable interest is, ''May I humbly enquire what you'll deign to eat today, and when should I prepare it?'' Or, ''What time should I awaken you in the morning, and would you like me to drive you to work?'' Intrusion is, ''Where are you going and what time will you be home?'''

Lee laughed at his clowning, but she could sense the vein of seriousness beneath it as well, and she was glad. If Daniel had really learned to tread carefully with his daughter things might yet come right for them.

His next words seemed to prove it. 'And by going softly I actually get told quite a lot.'

'You applied the scholar's brain to the problem, huh?'

'No, it was you,' he said. 'You showed me the way. Bless you, Lee. Everything's going to be fine, thanks to you.'

He drew her close. 'They'll be here in a minute,' she murmured.

'Then kiss me quickly,' he said against her lips.

The sound of the key turning in the front door made them spring apart self-consciously. There came the sound of urgent whispering from the hall, then Phoebe and Mark came in together, their arms entwined, their eyes shining. Phoebe threw herself forward into her father's arms.

'Oh, Daddy, I'm so happy,' she said ecstatically.

'That's wonderful, darling. Is it anything special? A new assignment?'

'No, it's much better than that. We're engaged.'

Daniel stiffened. 'What did you say?'

'Mark and I are going to be married. He asked me this afternoon and he's given me the most beautiful engagement ring. Look.'

She held up her left hand to show off the ring that flashed there. Daniel stared at it for a moment. Then he said in a hard voice, 'Take it off.'

'Daddy?' Phoebe backed away, startled by the instant change that had come over her father.

'Take it off. Now. And forget any idea of an engagement. You're sixteen, for Pete's sake! What's got into you?'

'I'm in love,' she cried. 'And I'm going to be married.'

'Over my dead body.'

'You can't stop me,' Phoebe said defiantly.

Daniel's face set. 'I'll stop you if I have to lock you in this house until you see sense.'

'Daniel, be careful,' Lee said warningly. She could have wept with despair at the way all his new-found subtlety had deserted him in this crisis. He was once more the autocratic patriarch who'd learned nothing.

He rounded on her. 'Don't say you approve of this. Why don't you tell that feather-brained daughter of mine what happens to girls who marry at sixteen?'

'Because you're not letting anyone else get a word in edgeways,' Lee cried. 'I'm as appalled as you are, but this isn't the way.'

'Then tell me what the way is,' he said through gritted teeth. 'Tell me how to get some sense into a girl who's been given too much of her own way too soon and thinks she can do any damned thing she wants.' Before Lee could answer he'd swung back to Phoebe. 'I told you to take that ring off,' he said in a biting voice.

'I won't. It's mine. I don't have to do what you want.'

'The hell you don't!'

'Don't talk to her like that,' Mark said.

Daniel seemed to notice him for the first time. 'I might have known it would be you who'd cause all the trouble,' he said. 'You've been bad news from the first. Who do you think you are to want to marry my daughter? A student who hasn't even finished his education. What are you going to live on—or didn't you bother to think about anything so mundane?'

'I'm making enough for both of us—' Phoebe said.

'So you're going to live off your wife,' Daniel demanded of Mark in a voice full of contempt.

'I won't need to,' Mark told him. 'I've got money of my own. It'll support us until I'm earning.'

'Sure it will. All of fourpence a week.'

'A bit more than that actually,' Mark said. 'Why don't you ask Lee the exact amount? She's my trustee.'

Under Daniel's hard gaze Lee coloured and said, 'Dad left Mark thirty thousand pounds two years ago. With interest, it's grown.'

He stared at her. 'But you wouldn't let him have it now? It's unthinkable.'

'Of course not.'

'Once I'm married she'll have no choice,' Mark said.

'So there's nothing to stop us,' Phoebe said.

'Now there you're wrong, young woman,' Daniel told her. 'I will stop you, and make no mistake. I mean every word. Give him that ring back.'

'No,' she whispered.

'Give it back.'

'Daniel, don't!' Lee said desperately. 'It doesn't make any difference whether she returns the ring or not. It isn't a ring that makes an engagement.'

Daniel flung her a black look. It held the same condemnation she'd seen that first time, when Phoebe had defied him about modelling, only now it was far worse.

'All right,' he said quietly. 'I'll deal with that later.' He turned on Mark. 'Get out of my house. And stay out. Don't come near my daughter again if you know what's good for you.'

'Go home, Mark,' Lee said.

'Not while Phoebe wants me,' he said firmly.

'Please go, Mark,' Phoebe said through her tears. 'I'll see you tomorrow.'

Lee saw Daniel's face tighten, but before he could speak she silenced him with a warning shake of the head. Phoebe fled the room, and after a moment Lee followed her upstairs. She found her lying full length across her bed, sobbing bitterly.

'I hate Daddy,' she choked. 'Why can't he understand?'

'But he does,' Lee told her, sitting down and patting her shoulder. 'He understands all sorts of things that you don't know about. He doesn't want you to get hurt.'

'Your dad's only trying to do what's best for you, love,' was what her mother had said.

'But I love Mark. I want to marry him and be with him for ever,' Phoebe cried.

'I love Jimmy...I'll always love him...' How the wheel turned full circle, and words spoken in passion came back to haunt her!

'Phoebe, you're sixteen and Mark's nineteen. In a few years you'll be different people. You don't know what you'll feel then.'

'You're just saying that to stop me. But *you* said I was entitled to make my own decisions.'

'In your career, not about marriage.'

'Oh, Lee, I thought *you'd* understand. You married at my age—'

'That's why I don't want to see you make a mess of your life as I did. It was a terrible mistake. The biggest mistake I ever made.'

'But you had the courage to follow your heart,' Phoebe cried. 'I've always admired you for that.'

Lee sighed and buried her head in her hands. After a moment she looked up and said quietly, 'It wasn't courage. It was stupidity. The only good thing to come out of my marriage was Sonya. The rest was a nightmare.'

'But Mark and I are different,' Phoebe said, using the age-old words.

'Maybe you are, but it won't hurt to wait a bit. It wasn't very kind to hurl it at your father like a bombshell. Cool it for a while, for his sake.'

'He had no right to tell me to give my ring back.'

Lee looked at the ring sparkling on the girl's finger. It was a beautiful creation of rubies and diamonds.

Dismayed, Lee put its price at around a thousand pounds. So that was where Mark's extra credit had gone.

'If you love Mark, you won't want to hurt him,' she suggested. 'He got into serious debt to buy this, and it's going to be a struggle for him to pay it off.'

Phoebe looked stricken. 'I didn't think.'

'Give it back, Phoebe. Not because your father says so, but for Mark's sake.'

'But we're still engaged.'

'Well, as I told your father, a ring doesn't make an engagement. It's what's in the heart that does that. If you love Mark, you can wait until he's finished his degree. You don't want to blight his career just when yours is taking off.'

'Of course not. I didn't mean we were going to get married tomorrow, and I'd have said so if Daddy hadn't started acting like a dictator.'

'Just be nice to him. Remember, time's on your side.'

When she went downstairs a few minutes later she found Daniel alone. He scowled at her.

'Phoebe's going to return the ring the next time she sees Mark,' she said.

'She's never seeing him again,' Daniel said at once. 'You can take it back to him yourself, and tell him this so-called engagement is off.'

Lee took a deep breath. 'Phoebe isn't calling the engagement off. She's returning the ring for Mark's sake, because she knows he can't afford it. She's also ready to wait until he finishes his degree. Nothing has really changed, Daniel.'

'Nothing—?'

'If you'd let Phoebe get a word in edgeways she'd have told you that they're not planning an immediate marriage. When things have calmed down they'll get the chance to see each other clearly, and the whole thing will die a natural death.' She saw that he was still looking at her with a black, frozen look on his face, and something painful happened to her heart.

'That's your advice, is it?' he asked coldly.

'For what it's worth, yes.'

'I just stand back and watch my daughter sleepwalk to disaster—?'

'Give them time and the marriage will never happen. There doesn't have to be a disaster—unless you drive her to it by bullying her.'

'Is it bullying to want to save her from herself?'

'That depends on how you do it,' she said slowly.

'Thank you,' he snapped. 'I know how to take that, I suppose.'

'Let's not talk about this any more today,' Lee said quietly. 'It's too dangerous.'

'Lee, just how long do you think we can go on not talking about the things that matter?'

'I don't know. I hoped it would all come right, but it seems to get worse and worse.'

Daniel didn't answer this directly. He was silent for a moment, then he said, 'I heard what she said to you just now.'

'What?'

'I came up to see her. I heard her say that you'd had the courage to follow your heart, and that was why she'd always admired you.'

'I told her it wasn't courage but stupidity,' Lee said quickly. 'Didn't you hear that?'

'No, you spoke so quietly that I couldn't hear, and after that I went away.'

'I told her my marriage was the biggest mistake I ever made!' Lee cried.

'Yes, I dare say you did. But just the same—'

'Daniel, what is it?'

'What kind of influence are you having on my daughter? Why couldn't you have helped me control her properly in the first place, instead of going against me?'

'I never went against you, Daniel,' Lee said, very pale. 'I only tried to show you that the kind of control you wanted wasn't possible any more. I tried to stop you losing her.'

'But I *am* losing her.'

'And you blame me?'

'No,' he said, too quickly. 'Of course not. It's just that I—I can't help thinking how things could have been different.'

'Different but for me, you mean? Different if you'd never met me at all? That's what you're thinking, isn't it? *If only I'd never met her!*'

'Stop it!' he said harshly. 'You're right. We mustn't say any more.'

'But you said it was time we had it out.'

'I didn't say exactly that—'

'"How long do you think we can go on not talking about the things that matter?"' she quoted back at him. 'And *why* don't we talk about them? Because it would finish us. What kind of relationship exists only because we hide from the truth? And the truth is that you blame me for everything that's happened. Why don't you admit it?'

He didn't speak, but it was there in his eyes.

Lee knew she should have kept quiet, but she was at the end of her tether. A demon seemed to be lashing her on to say terrible, irrevocable things.

'Say it,' she told him. 'Say you wish you'd never met me, because without me you needn't have faced the fact that Phoebe is growing up. Without me you could have kept her a prisoner for ever—'

'That's enough!' His voice crashed into her, thunderous with rage. 'You were right. How can we ever be together when we can do nothing but hurt each other?'

'Then let's end it now,' she choked.

'If that's what you want.'

'I do,' she cried. 'I love you, Daniel, but I can't take this any more. I can't be the whipping girl whenever life doesn't do what you want. I'm sorry. I tried. But I can't see things as you do, and I never will.'

'Lee—' He put out a hand to stop her as she moved to the door. The truth about what was happening seemed to get through to him. 'Don't go yet.'

'What's the point in staying?' she asked passionately. 'We both know how it would end at last. So let it end now.'

'It can't end,' he said harshly. 'We love each other.'

'I guess that just isn't enough. We're not adolescents to believe that love solves all problems. We're old enough to know that some problems *can't* be solved. Let me go, Daniel. We can only hurt each other.'

'Lee—*Lee*!' He reached out but she backed away.

'And I'll tell you this, Daniel, however much you

wish we'd never met, it can't be as much as I wish it.'

'You don't mean that,' he said.

'I do. I *do*! I was content, I had a good life, I was safe. You took it all away from me. Don't come after me, *please*. Just forget about me.'

She ran out of the house. She had no car tonight because Daniel had collected her from home, but after a moment she saw Mark's car in the street. He was standing beside it.

'What is it?' he asked as she ran up to him.

'Take me home, Mark,' she choked.

As the car swung round she saw Daniel standing in the window. She covered her face. Once before she'd promised herself never to see him again. She knew now she should have stuck to that vow. But this time she meant it. And one day, far in the future, perhaps her heart would stop breaking.

In their first quarrel Daniel had refused to accept that anything could come between them. This time it was different, and she realised that he too had faced the inevitable. She told herself she was glad that he'd seen sense, but she'd more than half expected him to come after her, and his silence was like a blow.

Now all her information about him and Phoebe came at second hand. She knew Daniel hadn't carried out his wild threat to lock his daughter up because Mark went out one evening to keep a date with her. He returned late that night in a black mood.

'I suppose I have you to thank, haven't I?' he demanded.

'For what, love?'

'This,' he said bitterly, holding the ring up. 'Phoebe returned this and said I should take it back to the shop.'

'Did she say why?'

'Oh, yes. She talked about waiting until I could afford it. She said she couldn't let me get into debt because of her. In fact, she sounded exactly like you.'

'Phoebe's a sensible girl—' Lee began to say, but Mark interrupted her furiously.

'Did you tell her I couldn't afford this ring?'

'Yes, because it's true.'

'Well, thank you very much for humiliating me. I suppose it's no more than I might have expected. Money, money, money! That's all you think matters. You don't care about love.'

'Oh, yes,' she murmured, 'I care about love very much.'

'You don't know what love is, Lee. If you did, you'd have stopped playing with Mr Raife and married him long ago. Phoebe says he's half off his head with your tricks.'

'That's not fair!' she cried.

'All I know is that I've had enough. I'm getting out of this house tonight. You've interfered in my life for the last time.'

He was as good as his word. Ignoring her pleas, he departed within the hour and moved in with a college friend. Lee was left to mull over his words. She rejected them. She knew they were unjust. But they left an uneasy residue in her mind.

A phone call to Brenda Mulroy told her that Phoebe was still working.

'But she's not well,' Brenda confided. 'She's told

me a little of what's happened. I think the atmosphere is pretty difficult at home, and she looks as if she's spent a lot of time crying. I've told her if she goes about with red eyes she won't get the Linnon contract.'

'Linnon?' Lee echoed, startled. The Linnon Corporation manufactured very expensive cosmetics and were about to launch a new line.

'They're thinking of using Phoebe as "the face",' Brenda said excitedly. 'It's not final, but I'm pretty sure. It'll absolutely make her.'

Lee made a real effort to put both Daniel and Phoebe out of her mind and give Sonya more of her attention. Her daughter was being a tower of strength, supporting her mother's spirits as no thirteen-year-old should have to do. When she tried to put on a cheerful face Sonya merely said gently, 'It's all right, Mum. You don't have to pretend for me.'

Lee was awoken one morning by the ringing of the telephone. It seemed to have an urgent sound, and afterwards she fancied that it had held a warning of the dreadful news that was to come.

'Hello?'

'Lee? It's Daniel. Is your brother there?'

'No, Mark doesn't live here now. He moved out a couple of weeks ago.'

He made a sound under his breath. 'Then it's no use asking if you know where Phoebe is?'

'Phoebe? Isn't she with you?'

'No. She's not in her room and there was a note on her pillow.'

CHAPTER ELEVEN

DANIEL looked thinner and desperately strained when he arrived at Lee's home. He followed her into the kitchen and held out Phoebe's letter for Lee to read.

> Daddy darling,
>
> Please try to understand and not be too angry. I love Mark and we have to be together. So we are going to be married in Gretna Green, like Lee. Don't try to stop us, because we belong together.
>
> Phoebe.

Lee read it, her heart thumping painfully. The words 'going to be married in Gretna Green, like Lee' seemed to stand out accusingly.

'She came home early yesterday evening,' Daniel said. 'The atmosphere between us seemed better than it's been for a long time. She insisted on cooking supper for me. We talked, she was sweet and delightful, it was like old times. I thought I was getting through to her at last—' His voice became husky. Lee reached out a hand to him but he shook his head.

'Actually she was saying goodbye,' he said eventually. 'She had it all planned to run away while I was asleep.' He gave a short, mirthless laugh. 'The condemned man was being given a hearty meal. She even kissed me goodnight. It's a long time since she's done that. And all the time...'

'I can't believe this,' Lee murmured. 'Oh, the silly girl!'

'So much for her taking her career seriously! She's got work lined up. How can she do it if she's living in Scotland, establishing residence?'

'She doesn't have to,' Lee said, trying to pull herself together. 'We thought that, too—Jimmy and I—but he found out you can organise it by post. You have to give fifteen days notice, but you needn't get there until the last minute. Mark could have arranged it from where he's living now.' A sudden thought made her ask sharply, 'When's Phoebe's next booking?'

'Thursday,' he said, growing pale. 'And this is Monday.'

'Then they've fixed it for tomorrow or the day after.'

'I'm going to stop that wedding if it's the last thing I do. And you're coming with me.'

She gasped. 'Oh, no, Daniel, please. I can't go back there.'

'You must,' he said. 'You know the place.'

'But I don't,' she cried desperately. 'I've blotted it all out of my memory.'

'Lee, I need you. It'll all come back to you. It *must*. I'm racing against time. You could save me vital minutes. *Please*.'

A thousand painful ghosts seemed to scream a warning at her. 'I can't leave Sonya alone in the house,' she said desperately.

'Then we'll take her with us.'

'She has to go to school.'

'I see what it is,' he said coldly. 'You're afraid,

and your fear is more important than anything else, isn't it? More important than Phoebe, than me—'

'No!'

'And you'll go on being afraid to the end of your days because you never had the courage to confront it. All right. Keep your refuge. Hide away in it. Much good it will do you.'

His tone stung her, forcing her to see what she'd always avoided before. *There's no safe place in love.* And this was Daniel, whom she loved despite everything. His face was ravaged, terrible.

'It's all right,' she said. 'I'm coming with you.'

He regarded her steadily. 'Thank you,' he said at last. 'I'll collect you here in an hour.' He left without another word.

It was arranged that Sonya should stay with Katie, her best friend at school. Lee got on the phone to Katie's mother, then to Gillian to rearrange her schedule for the following week. Luckily she'd left herself a few days free to catch up with paperwork.

'But you really have to be back for Thursday,' Gillian said. 'You're doing a big shoot for *Vogue.* We've got six models booked and a very tight deadline. If you let them down it'll set you back years.'

'I'll be there,' Lee promised. 'I should know one way or the other by tomorrow.'

Daniel arrived, looking more tense than ever. 'Look what arrived in the post a few minutes ago,' he said, holding out a glossy magazine.

'Woman Of The World,' Lee said, stunned. 'That's Phoebe on the front cover.'

It was the final shot from the wedding session:

Phoebe in the simple gown and veil, looking ravishing.

'The front cover!' Lee breathed.

'Yes, I imagine you're delighted,' Daniel said grimly.

'Of course I am. It's a marvellous start for her. Daniel, don't you see that this proves I was right about her potential, that *she* was right to follow her dream?'

'In fact, everyone was right except me?' he said bitterly.

'Yes. I think you should admit now that you were wrong.'

'Should I? Then let me remind you that this—' he tapped the picture '—was the first step on the road to Gretna Green and a disastrous marriage to a young man as callow as he's selfish.'

'They're not married yet. We can still prevent it.'

'That would be easier if we knew when it's going to be. I called the register office up there a few minutes ago—I thought I could find out the time of the wedding, but they don't give out that kind of information. It's posted up outside, but that's all.'

'PI,' said Sonya.

The other two stared at her. 'PI,' she repeated. 'Private investigator. Find the Yellow Pages for that area in the library. It'll list the local PIs. Then you call one and he goes down and reads what's written outside the register office. You could know in a couple of hours.'

'Sonya, you're a genius,' Daniel said fervently. 'Where's your local library?'

She gave him directions and he vanished.

'Well done, darling,' Lee said. 'Where would we be without you?' Something impelled her to add, 'Daniel's sister Jean said you get your brains from me.'

Sonya grinned, understanding this perfectly, and went to make a cup of tea. The phone rang and Lee snatched it up. It was Brenda Mulroy.

'Do you know where Phoebe is?' she asked urgently. 'I've called her home but there's no reply.'

'But—surely she's free until Thursday?'

'Yes, but I've heard from the Linnon people. They've decided to offer her the contract to be the face of Linnon.'

'That's marvellous!'

'Isn't it just? But they want another meeting with her, quickly, and I can't find her.'

Lee's brain raced. 'I don't know exactly where she is at this moment,' she declared, with perfect truth.

'A phone number?'

'I think she wanted to use her free days to get away from it all—out of reach of a phone,' Lee said, improvising wildly.

'It's not very professional of her to do that just now.'

'She probably didn't think she was this close to the Linnon contract.'

'Hmm! I hope you marry Phoebe's father soon. You'll be a steadying influence on her. If you hear from her, tell her to call me.' Brenda hung up.

Lee took a few deep breaths to steady her nerves. The shocks of the morning had left her wondering—what next?

After a few minutes Daniel returned. 'I got a little

firm ten miles away from Gretna,' he said. 'Someone's going along to check. I've given him the number of my carphone. Let's go. What's the matter?'

'I'll tell you on the way.'

They dropped Sonya off at Katie's house. She hugged them both in farewell, and something fell out of her bag.

'You're a bit old for plasticine, aren't you?' Lee asked as Sonya hurriedly retrieved the object.

'It's for a very serious purpose,' Sonya said, stuffing it back into the bag.

'What serious purpose?'

'I'm going to make an effigy of Mark and stick pins into it.'

'Stick one in for me,' Daniel said grimly.

'Bye, you two,' Sonya said, and waved as they drove off.

When they'd turned the corner Lee let out her breath. In the flurry of departure she'd had little time to realise that she was going to be alone with Daniel.

Neither of them spoke at first. He was following the route she'd taken fourteen years ago, out of London to Birmingham and then Carlisle, but she felt it was too soon to be troubled. She'd driven this way herself several times to do location work. It was only after Birmingham that the past would start to trouble her.

'What were you going to tell me?' he asked as they swung onto the motorway and left London behind.

'Brenda called, looking for Phoebe. The Linnon Corporation have offered her a contract. I told her Phoebe was having a short break, "away from it all".

I hope we find her quickly. If she doesn't call Brenda back soon it'll look bad.'

'What difference does it make? You don't think I'm going to let her accept, do you? It's time this whole business was brought to an end.'

Lee remained silent. It was useless pointing out to Daniel that Phoebe's career was way beyond his control. In his heart he knew it. His words were cries in the dark from a man who hadn't come to terms with the situation. She took out *Woman Of The World* and studied the cover again, feeling a deep professional satisfaction in having discovered this perfect material and having brought out the best in her.

And there was more inside. Lindsay Elwes had been so stunned by Phoebe that she'd included a short feature about 'the face of the future'. Every word was designed to send Phoebe further up the ladder of success and to break Daniel's heart.

The carphone rang and Daniel snatched it up. He listened, his face dark, and grunted his thanks before he hung up.

'Well?' Lee asked.

'About as bad as it can be. They're the first wedding tomorrow morning.'

'Oh, heavens!'

'I'm running low on petrol. I'll stop at the next service station and fill up.'

At the services they stretched their legs and had coffee. They sat in virtual silence. Lee's heart was heavy as she realised they were like strangers. Once she met his eyes and looked away quickly, but not before she saw him do the same.

When they resumed travelling her memories grew

sharper. She couldn't recall the scenery. It was the distances that counted. Fifty miles out of London, then sixty. At this stage she'd been spending the journey twisted around in her seat, anxiously watching the road behind for any sign of her parents' car, until Jimmy had told her to stop being daft.

A hundred miles. They'd stopped for something to eat. She'd brought some money with her, but not as much as Jimmy had expected. He'd been snappy and irritable, which she'd ascribed to nerves. Later she was to learn that Jimmy was always irritable when he didn't get exactly what he wanted.

After their next stop Lee suggested to Daniel that she should take a turn at driving. He agreed, but it wasn't a success. His state of the art, computerised vehicle needed practice. Lee fumbled uneasily and finally settled into the slow lane until the next exit, when she gladly returned it to him.

'Sorry,' she said, cross with herself.

'Don't be. It wasn't your fault. I shouldn't have agreed.'

'You're going to be so tired if you have to do it all yourself.'

'Don't worry about me. We're making good time.'

It was a fatal thing to say. Almost at once the traffic slowed and in a few minutes they'd come to a standstill. Lee groaned at the sight of a jam stretching as far as her eyes could see.

After that they moved at a crawl for the next three hours. Now was another chance to talk. Lee waited, longing for Daniel to begin, but he only switched the radio on. After all, she thought, what was there to say?

At last they could move freely again, but they'd

lost precious hours and the light was fading fast. As they went further north the rain started to fall, softly at first but then harder, until they were driving through a downpour.

'We've got to stop somewhere,' Lee said. 'You've driven nearly three hundred miles and you're exhausted. If we keep on through this we're going to have an accident.'

'I want to get there tonight,' Daniel said stubbornly. 'We might find out where they're staying.'

'They may not be in Gretna Green at all,' Lee protested. 'They might go straight to Gretna, which is next door. The register office is there. Let's spend the night in Carlisle. That's what Jimmy and I did. It's only nine miles away, and if we put up at a hotel there we can still get to Gretna before the register office opens. *Don't pull out!*'

Daniel swore and drew back just in time as a juggernaut thundered past him.

'I didn't see him,' he admitted. 'All right. We'll stay overnight in Carlisle.'

They stopped at the first hotel they came to. It was a small place, slightly shabby but cosy and friendly. While Daniel brought in the bags Lee booked two single rooms. She knew she'd been right to insist on stopping. Daniel's face was grey with strain and weariness.

'I'll call Room Service for a snack and then turn in,' he said.

'I'm afraid this hotel doesn't have Room Service,' Lee told him. 'We'll have to go downstairs.'

'I'll fall asleep over the soup.'

'I won't let you,' she promised. 'Come on.'

They secured the last table in the restaurant and ate without speaking until the main course was over. Once Daniel glanced up, smiled briefly and looked away again.

'I feel more human now,' he admitted. 'I've booked an early call tomorrow, so we'll have time to get there.'

'Daniel, what are you going to do when we meet them?'

'Don't worry, I'm not going to make a scene. I'll just tell Phoebe very calmly that I've come to take her home.'

'And suppose she won't go with you?'

'She'll have to. She's got to see sense about this.'

'But if she won't? What are you going to do? Drag her to the car?'

'It won't come to that.'

'But if it does?'

'Lee, please, don't push me now. I'm not in complete control of my temper.'

And not to be in control was something he hated. Lee gave up the attempt. Tomorrow would bring whatever it brought. She could only hope Daniel showed more wisdom in handling his daughter than he had so far.

As they were getting ready to leave the table a hesitant voice halted them. 'Forgive me, but—you are Daniel Raife, aren't you?'

He raised his head with a look of impatience, which faded as he saw an elderly lady, her hands clutched tightly together. Her face was a mixture of nervousness and determination, as though she'd had to force herself to speak.

'Yes, I am,' Daniel admitted with a tired smile.

'Do forgive me for— That is, I know you must hate people forcing themselves on you—but you're the only person who could help me. I don't know where else to turn.'

Without hesitation Daniel pulled over a free chair and waved the old woman into it with his most delightful smile. Lee, who knew the state he was in, marvelled at the self-control that enabled him to brush his own feelings aside.

'Tell me about it,' he said.

The story came out haltingly. Her name was Mrs Myra Hallam and just over a year ago her husband had been knocked down and killed by a drunk driver. The driver had subsequently been fined two hundred and fifty pounds.

'It was like saying all Freddy was worth was two hundred and fifty pounds,' Mrs Hallam said, in tears. 'If the man had been properly punished—it wouldn't have brought Freddy back, but it would have done him justice. But this—' She buried her face in her hands for a moment, then made an effort to recover herself.

'Now all I want to do is tell people. It happens all the time—drunks who kill people and get off lightly. I never understood before—it's got to be stopped. People have got to be told. And you can tell them. Your show...'

Lee was wrung with pity for her, especially as she knew Daniel had already covered a similar theme recently on the show, and that his producer wouldn't look at it again for a long time. She wondered how he would manage to break the truth to her.

Then she realised that the old lady had gone back to the beginning and was telling the story again. Daniel showed no sign of impatience but sat with his hand enfolding hers, watching her with eyes that were gentle. Even when everything was repeated a third time his perfect kindness and courtesy never failed him.

'Look,' he said at last, bringing a notebook from his pocket, 'give me your phone number. I've already used this subject on the show, and it'll be a while before I can touch it again on television, but I can write about it. I'll call you in a few days and we can have a proper talk then.'

'Oh, thank you. You're so kind.'

'I wish I could do more,' he said.

'But you've helped so much—just listening to me. It's the only thing I can do for Freddy, you see, tell his story.'

Daniel hailed a waiter and ordered three coffees. 'I'll just be a moment,' he said, rising. 'I want to pay the bill so that we can leave early.'

He hurried out to Reception, leaving Lee alone with Mrs Hallam.

'I'm afraid I've rambled on rather,' the old lady confided. 'But I can't help brooding about it, especially just now, because next week would have been our wedding anniversary. We would have been married fifty-one years.'

'Oh, no!' Lee exclaimed. 'You mean he died just before your Golden Wedding?'

'Yes. You know, nobody expected our marriage to be a success—we were so different. But I think that was why it worked so well. Where one was foolish, the other was wise, and so we helped each other.

'It was the night before our Golden Wedding and I had a big surprise planned for him. He kept trying to find out. I told him to go out to the pub and stop trying to peek. I even got a little cross with him because I was afraid the surprise would be spoiled. So he went out that night and—and he didn't come back. He never got to see the surprise at all.'

Lee could only look at her in sympathy, her own eyes filled with tears.

'I'll always regret it,' Mrs Hallam said simply. 'I was so busy worrying about tomorrow that I neglected today. Now I know that today is all we're ever sure of. But it's too late. Perhaps everyone learns that too late.'

In the distance they could see Daniel returning. Mrs Hallam blew her nose and forced herself to speak brightly. 'I was really nervous about approaching him. He seems very pleasant on television, only you wonder what people are like when the cameras are off. But he really is a nice man, isn't he?'

'Yes,' Lee agreed quietly. 'He really is a nice man.'

Lee thought she was sure to fall asleep at once, but despite her tiredness she lay awake for hours that night. Mrs Hallam's words tormented her: 'I was so busy worrying about tomorrow that I neglected today...today is all we're ever sure of...everyone learns that too late.'

She'd refused to commit herself to her love, asking for some kind of guarantee for the future before she did so. But there were no guarantees. There were only risks. But it was love that gave you the courage to take those risks.

She loved Daniel. That was the only certainty. But she'd allowed fear to overcome her, as though fear were more important than love. And because her courage had failed she hadn't been the woman Daniel needed in his hour of crisis.

Brenda had said, 'I hope you marry Phoebe's father soon. You'll be a steadying influence on her.'

Daniel had sometimes blamed her unjustly, but he'd never thrown at her the accusation she now threw at herself: if she'd married him when he'd first asked she could have steered him clear of this disaster. She would have been living with him and Phoebe these last few weeks and then, she was sure, things would never have come to this pass.

He'd begged her to be his wife, out of love but also out of need. Some instinct had told him that she was the woman who could guide him away from the pitfalls. But she'd abandoned him in his need, leaving him to make mistake after mistake, with no one to help him.

Mrs Hallam had known the secret. 'Where one was foolish, the other was wise, and so we helped each other.' It was so simple really.

At last Lee rose, slipped on her dressing gown and went out into the corridor. His room was next to hers. She paused outside his door, her hand uplifted to knock, but after a moment she went in without knocking. She knew he wouldn't be asleep.

He was sitting at the window. He turned as she entered and watched her cautiously, never taking his eyes from her as she approached.

'I came because I had something to tell you,' she said. She stopped. Her heart was beating too fast.

She'd meant to speak the thoughts that had troubled her, perhaps say that she was sorry. But the misery on his face wiped everything else out. What she had to say was far more simple.

'I love you,' she said, and felt his arms go about her in a passion of thankfulness.

For a long time they held each other tightly, in silence. There was nothing more to say. His head found its place against her breast, where she cradled it tenderly. He was hers, for good or ill. He wasn't perfect, but neither was she. And he loved her with a commitment and honesty that Jimmy Meredith would never have understood.

She spared one final, fleeting thought for Jimmy, the malign presence who had almost ruined her life. Then she banished him for ever.

'Come, my love,' she whispered, taking Daniel's hand and leading him to the bed. It was here they would find each other again.

She'd made love to Daniel many times with passion, but tonight her overwhelming emotion was a desire to protect him. She hadn't known before that he needed protecting, but she knew it now, and with every caress, every whispered word, she let him know that she was his, in any way that he needed her.

She, too, sought reassurance in their loving. She wanted to know that after all the bitterness that had passed between them he was still hers, and the promise was given back to her a thousandfold. Once before they'd clung to each other, shocked by their first quarrel. But this wasn't like that time. Then they'd tried to hide from the knowledge of their differences. Now those differences had translated into mutual need, and they were the stronger for it.

They loved each other deeply, intimately. The moonlight coming through the window lit their faces and the smiles of thankfulness that they shared. When at last they nestled against each other he held her tight, as if he would never let her go.

'I know the truth about myself now,' he said sombrely. 'And it isn't pleasant.'

'Daniel—don't.'

'I'm a bully, aren't I?'

'No. It's not like that.'

'I'm a bully and I drove Phoebe away. If she makes a mess of her life it will be my fault. *Help me, Lee.*'

'Always, darling.'

'Don't go away again where I can't find you.'

'I'll never leave you now.'

'Then perhaps there's hope for me.'

'Go to sleep,' she whispered. 'We have to be up early.'

He was asleep before she'd finished speaking, as though he now had all he needed. His head was heavy against her breast and she stroked his hair lovingly. Whatever tomorrow might bring they had found each other again, and this time she was determined that nothing should drive them apart. Her eyes began to grow heavy as she listened to the soft rhythm of his breathing. Peace. Love. All was well.

CHAPTER TWELVE

LEE awoke to the sound of running water and realised that Daniel was showering in the tiny bathroom. She yawned and stretched, feeling strong and well for the first time in weeks.

The telephone rang and she answered it, remembering the early call Daniel had booked. 'Thank you,' she murmured sleepily.

'Daniel Raife, please,' said a cool female voice.

She woke up. 'I'm afraid Daniel isn't available at the moment.'

The woman gave a 'tut' of annoyance. 'He wouldn't be! How familiar this is! Never there when you want him.'

'Excuse me, but who is this?'

'Caroline Jenkins. *Ms.* He left a message and I'm returning his call. Look, please tell him that I can be reached on this number—three, five, seven—'

'Hold on a moment.'

'Aren't you taking it down?'

'I will when I've got a pencil.' Lee found one and began to write. 'Three, five—'

Caroline Jenkins dictated the number slowly, as if dealing with an idiot. 'Are you sure you've got that?' she asked at last.

'Quite sure,' Lee said crisply.

'You'd better read it back to me. I don't want any mistakes.'

Lee did so, striving not to sound as annoyed as she felt.

'I'll be here for an hour,' Caroline Jenkins informed her. 'After that he can get me at home.'

'Does he know your home number?'

'Of course he does. Don't forget, will you?' She hung up.

Lee stared at the phone until enlightenment finally dawned.

'Good heavens!' she exclaimed. '*Caroline.* Phoebe's mother!'

Daniel emerged from the bathroom, wrapped in a towel. 'Was that our call?' he asked.

'No, it was Caroline. She said you'd left her a message to call here.'

'She left *me* a message on my answering machine. I called her back last night but she was out, so I left this number. I suppose I'd better find out what she wants.'

'Then you didn't call her to tell her about this?'

'No.' Daniel gave a wry grimace. 'I suppose I should have done, but I didn't want to give her the satisfaction. She's never thought much of me as a parent.' He began to dial.

'Shall I leave?'

'Why? So that I can talk privately to a woman I haven't seen in the flesh for over two years? Stay with me, darling. I need you.' He was dialling as he spoke.

'Hello, Caroline? Daniel here. Why did you call me?' A burst of high-pitched talk, like gunfire, came from the receiver. Daniel listened with his face settling into a scowl. 'Hell!' he said at last. 'Yes, of course I've seen it. I didn't know that you... No, I wasn't concealing it, I just didn't think you'd be interested, frankly.'

He put his hand over the mouthpiece and turned to Lee. 'Someone faxed her that magazine piece about Phoebe, and she's foaming at the mouth. Yes...?' He returned his attention to the phone from which more angry sounds were emerging. 'Caroline, there's no need to read it to me. I've read it myself.' He sighed and held out the receiver for Lee to listen. Caroline was going through the piece very slowly, emphasising certain words on a note of outrage.

'How could you let this happen?' she shrieked.

Daniel took a deep breath, and Lee thought he would explode. 'Let it happen?' he demanded at last, through gritted teeth. 'Let it happen? Now you listen to me, Caroline. I didn't "let it happen". It just happened because it had to happen. And you know what? I'm glad of it. I've always been proud of our daughter because she's brainy, but now I'm proud of her because she's beautiful, too. What's more, she's not only brainy and beautiful but she's got the guts to make her own life in her own way, and not feebly let us make it for her. *And that makes me prouder than anything.*' He slammed down the phone.

Lee burst into applause and threw her arms about him. 'My hero!' she exclaimed. 'Oh, Daniel, I'm so glad.'

He kissed her, then said reluctantly, 'I have to be honest. That woman can needle me into saying things I don't really mean. I'm not sure...'

'I don't believe it,' Lee said stubbornly. 'It's when you get good 'n' mad that the truth comes out.'

'Maybe. I'll know what the truth is when I see

Phoebe.' He drew her close, but almost immediately the phone shrilled again with their early call.

They took a quick breakfast and hurried out to the car. But at that point things began to go wrong. When Daniel turned the key in the ignition, nothing happened.

'My God! It won't start!' he said in horror.

He tried again and again, and finally got some result. But the car simply made revving noises, declining to spark into life.

'Oh, no!' Lee nearly wept. 'How can this happen?'

'Keep trying,' he said tersely, and leapt from the car.

Lee slid into the driving seat and spent several fruitless, agonising minutes without result. Daniel returned, looking tense.

'I've called a taxi,' he said. 'They promised to get here at once. We might just still make it.'

'I'm sorry,' she said frantically. 'If I hadn't made you stop here last night—'

'We'd have had an accident,' he said quickly. 'You did the right thing. If only that taxi gets here fast.'

But it didn't. It was twenty minutes before it arrived, and then the journey to Gretna seemed to take an age. Daniel fixed his gaze on his watch with terrible intensity, and Lee saw the hope drain out of his face.

'We're too late,' he said at last. 'They must have started by now. By the time we get there it will be over.'

When they reached the register office they found a little crowd outside, but no sign of Phoebe or Mark.

They exchanged looks of despair, knowing that this meant the worst.

'They're coming out,' said someone. 'Aren't they a lovely couple?'

Lee and Daniel looked up as the bride and groom emerged. The next moment they gasped.

'It's not them,' Lee said. 'I don't understand. They were booked first.'

She ran inside and found an official. 'Excuse me, was there another wedding before this?'

'No, this is the first one of the day,' he told her.

'But—Phoebe Raife and Mark Kendall...?'

'Oh, them. They put their wedding off until this afternoon. Luckily the next couple had just arrived, so it was easy to change it around.'

'Put it off?' she said, hardly daring to hope. 'Did they say why?'

'Well, they didn't seem exactly the best of friends at the time. The young lady was more than a wee bit cross.'

'Daniel,' Lee called, running out. 'It's all right. They've delayed the wedding until this afternoon. They've had some kind of tiff. If we can only find them first—'

'How?' He asked urgently.

She reached into her bag and pulled out the copy of *Woman Of The World* with Phoebe on the cover. 'Show people this picture and ask if they've seen her.'

He took the magazine from her. 'You know Gretna. Where would they go?'

For a moment, Lee's mind went blank and then it came back to her. Just before their wedding she and Jimmy had also had a tiff, and she'd run away to be by herself—'Sulking like a baby,' he'd sneered. Barely looking where she was going, she'd taken the little country path to Gretna Green, and found the old Smithy where she'd stood watching the guide explain to a party of tourists how the old marriages had once taken place.

'They clasped hands and claimed each other,' he'd said. 'And the blacksmith struck the anvil and cried, "So be it!"'

She'd brushed back her tears. This was her wedding day. Things were so different from her dream of a romantic elopement. Jimmy had been critical and impatient, and the truth about him had crept into her mind. If her parents had found her then, there would have been no wedding. Instead Jimmy had reached her first, and had been shrewd enough to sweet-talk her enough to get her back to the register office. And her parents had arrived too late…

'The smithy,' she said to Daniel now. 'Let's hurry.'

'But we'd have passed her on the road,' he said.

'Not if they took the country lane.'

They got into the car and in a few minutes were in the quiet little village of Gretna Green. Everywhere there were neat, white painted buildings surrounded by greenery and pale grey roads. The whole atmosphere was one of sleepy peacefulness that belied the desperate passion of young lovers and the frantic urgency of parents.

'The smithy's over there,' Lee said, pointing.

Hand in hand they ran across the grass to the long, low building. There was no one outside but they could hear the guide's voice and see a little crowd inside. They entered quietly and at once Daniel stiffened.

'There she is,' he muttered.

Phoebe was standing on the edge of the crowd, watching the little performance with a sad look on her face that Lee understood so well. She wore a dress and matching jacket of pale yellow. A little spray of flowers adorned her hair and she carried a small bouquet of flowers.

'She's alone,' Daniel whispered. 'You were right. We've won.'

She wanted to cry a warning. *Not yet! You haven't won yet. If you say the wrong thing now...* But it was too late. He could no longer hear her. Phoebe had seen them and turned to come out of the smithy. Her eyes were wary.

'Hello, Daddy,' she said, keeping her distance.

Daniel hesitated. 'I followed you,' he said, 'because—because I have something very important to say. I want you to know...' Almost unconsciously he was raising his hand, the one holding the magazine. 'I wanted to show you this, and to say—how very, very proud of you I am.'

As if by magic the defiance left Phoebe's face. 'Oh, *Daddy*!' she cried, bursting into tears, and threw herself into his arms. Daniel held her tightly, his eyes closed, giving silent thanks that the right words had come to him at last.

Phoebe released her father and looked at him with shining eyes. 'Are you really proud of me?' she asked eagerly. 'Really and truly?'

'Really and truly,' he promised. 'And look what it says inside.' He opened the magazine at the right page and Phoebe eagerly devoured the words about herself. 'There's something else too,' Daniel said. 'You've got the Linnon contract. Brenda wants you to call her at once.'

He was almost drowned out by Phoebe's squeal of delight. 'I've really got it? Oh, that's wonderful! A phone. I need a phone.'

'There's a hotel over there,' Lee said. 'They'll probably have a phone. Unless,' she added casually, 'you're waiting for Mark to join you here.'

The change that came over Phoebe was almost comical. She looked as if she'd only just remembered Mark's existence. 'No, he doesn't know I'm here. In fact I don't know where he is, either.'

'You can tell us about it over a cup of tea,' Daniel said. 'My poor darling, have you had a bad time?'

'Crawler,' Lee whispered to him.

'Low cunning,' he murmured back. 'Never fails.'

They ordered tea while Phoebe made her call. Daniel's whole being radiated suppressed triumph, and his eyes were tender as he gazed at his daughter. But out of sight he felt for Lee's hand and she could feel his shattering relief.

'Now tell us about Mark,' Daniel said, adding with foolhardy recklessness, 'Are we invited to the wedding?'

'Oh, Daddy! I don't want to marry Mark. I only ran away because—' She met his eyes.

'Because I hassled you?' he asked gently.

Phoebe nodded. 'I must have been crazy,' she admitted. 'Mark's even worse than you.'

'Thank you, darling,' Daniel said meekly.

'Oh, you know what I mean. The car broke down so we had to hire another one. Mark tried to pay with his credit card only there wasn't enough credit on it because he hadn't returned the ring, although he'd promised me. So we had an argument about that, and in the end I paid and that made him grumpy. I said there was no need to carry on about it because I had plenty of money now, and he just hated that. He sulked all the rest of the way.'

'Poor Phoebe,' Daniel said, fighting to keep a straight face.

'Honestly, Daddy, he's been the pits. I've decided to give up men altogether.'

'Well, some of them aren't all that bad,' Lee said, refusing to meet Daniel's eye. 'But you won't have time for them just now, with so many other horizons opening to you. Later, perhaps—'

'No, I'm giving them up for good,' Phoebe declared. 'I've got a life plan. I'm going to model for the next few years, maybe until I'm twenty-five. By then I'll be past my best, and I'll have made pots of money, and then I'll go to Oxford.'

'Oxford?' Daniel asked, hardly daring to hope.

'Of course. I always meant to go when I finished my modelling career.' She patted her father's hand kindly. 'I'll be ready for it by then.'

'But—why didn't you say so before?'

'I would have done if you'd given me the chance. But you kept laying down the law and making me cross, and by the time we'd finished bickering I'd forgotten what I wanted to say. But I'll go to Oxford in the end.'

'Only if you want to,' Daniel said quickly. 'It's your life and your choice.'

'Why did you postpone the wedding?' Lee asked.

'We just kept on niggling each other, and it didn't

seem right to marry like that. I guess I knew then that we weren't really going through with it. It was like a game, only then it became real, and suddenly I knew I didn't want to.'

Lee nodded silently. It had happened that way with her. But too late.

Daniel looked up. 'Ah! The groom.'

There was a scowl on Mark's face as he approached them. Daniel rose to his feet.

'I suppose you've talked her out of it,' Mark said sulkily.

'Phoebe didn't need any talking,' Lee told him. 'She knows neither of you are ready for marriage, and I think you know it too.'

'What I think,' he said furiously, 'is that none of this need have happened if you hadn't been so clutch-fisted with my money. It's all your fault, Lee, and if you had any sense of decency you'd—'

Mark never finished. Daniel's fist connected with his chin, sending him staggering back, clutching wildly at thin air. Lee and Phoebe got hastily out of the way while he collided with a low table and ended up sprawled on the sofa, looking up at his assailant with astonishment.

'Sorry,' Daniel said, blowing on his knuckles. 'I didn't mean to act like a caveman, but I don't allow anyone to insult my future wife.'

Phoebe beamed. 'That's wonderful! I'm so happy. I thought it would never happen.'

'But—' Lee began.

Daniel held up a hand—like a traffic cop, as his daughter later informed him. 'Lee, darling,' he said firmly, 'I could go grey-haired waiting for you to decide, and I don't intend to—certainly not after last night. I'm going to be very old-fashioned and tell you to stop dithering like some fluffy-headed little thing. I want to marry you and I'm tired of waiting. So you're going to give me an answer and then we're going to get married.'

'And my answer's going to be yes, is it?'

'It's the only answer I'll accept.' Daniel spoke calmly but his pallor betrayed his apprehension. 'I'm not much of a bargain as a husband. I'm overbearing, manipulative—all the things you've called me. But *I love you.* And you love me. Marriage is the only thing that makes sense. I want us to go into that smithy now and be married over the anvil.'

'But—but, Daniel,' she stammered, 'it won't be legally binding—'

'It doesn't matter. We'll have the official ceremony when we get back to London. But I want a smithy wedding, because I know that you'll never go back on anything you agree to in this place.'

Still she hesitated, longing for the courage to make the final leap. It had never occurred to her that Daniel would ask for her commitment here, of all places, where her ghosts lingered.

But that was why he'd done it, of course. It was there in his eyes: he knew exactly what she needed and how to care for her. With this one man she'd found not only love but also the security that had always eluded her. He'd said, 'There's no safe place in love', and it was true. But it was also true that the knowledge of love was the greatest safety, and it had taken her all this time to see it.

'I'll marry you,' she said joyfully, slipping her hand into his.

Phoebe let out a carol of delight, and even Mark grinned his pleasure. 'Sorry, Lee,' he said, and kissed her cheek.

'Here. You must have these.' Phoebe took the flowers from her hair and gently fitted them on Lee's head. Then she handed her the matching posy. 'Now you look like a bride.'

But it wasn't the flowers that made her look like a bride. It was the glow of happiness in her eyes as she gazed at Daniel, the second man she'd married in Gretna Green. And this time the right one.

He took her hand and they returned to the smithy. The tour guide had just finished with a party who were leaving. He smiled as he saw them, perfectly understanding the situation, and waved them forward.

'Are you sure?' Daniel asked anxiously.

'Quite sure,' Lee said fervently. 'Oh, my darling, I took far too long. But now I'm quite, quite sure.'

The anvil was there, the same anvil over which she'd made a terrible mistake a lifetime ago. But now everything was different. With Mark and Phoebe standing beside them they clasped hands, and Daniel spoke.

'I, Daniel, call on these persons here present to witness that I take Leonie to be my wife eternally.'

In a steady voice, Lee replied, 'I, Leonie, call on these persons here present to witness that I take Daniel to be my husband eternally.'

Then the guide raised his hammer to bring it thundering down onto the anvil, and in a loud voice he cried, *'So be it!'*